1896

LAST WAS LLOYD

OTHER YEARLING BOOKS YOU WILL ENJOY:

YEARLING BOOKS are designed especially to entertain and enlighten young people. Charles F. Reasoner, Professor of Elementary Education, New York University, is consultant to this series.

For a complete listing of all Yearling titles, write to Education Sales Department, Dell Publishing Co., Inc., 1 Dag Hammarskjold Plaza, New York, New York 10017.

Last Was Lloyd

Doris Buchanan Smith

A Yearling Book

Published by
Dell Publishing Co., Inc.
1 Dag Hammarskjold Plaza
New York, New York 10017

Yearling ® TM 913705, Dell Publishing Co., Inc.

ISBN: 0-440-44874-3

Reprinted by arrangement with The Viking Press

Printed in the United States of America

First Yearling printing—May 1982

CW

Randy,
this one is for you.

1

LAST WAS LLOYD.

When the captains came to the last person, no name was even called. Everyone knew. Last was Lloyd. The order of choosing teams depended on who had hit or fielded well the day before. Lloyd never had. When teams were chosen, all he had to do was pay enough attention to know which team had the next-to-last choice.

As his classmates sprinted toward the field, Lloyd fell in behind. For comfort, he slid his hand into his pocket and stroked the olive shell. The cool, slick smoothness and the sharp, spiraled point of the seashell's cone were familiar to his touch. The olive shell was his lucky piece, his reminder that there was a world away from school.

Being last choice, or rather no choice at all, he was also last batter. Today his team was hitting well, and he came up to bat in the second inning. Dangling a bat from his hand, he hung his head and shrugged his way to the batter's box, as though apologizing ahead of time. Before the first ball was pitched, his teammates were groaning and yelling.

"Don't swing at everything," they hollered as he swung widely at the first ball pitched.

"Swing, swing, swing," the opposing team chanted, and he swung widely as the second ball crossed the plate. On the third pitch he accidentally connected with the ball.

"Run, run, run!" his teammates yelled.

With the bat still in his hands, he stared stupidly after the ball. The ball bounded past the pitcher and plopped into the shortstop's glove.

"Run, run, run!" his teammates screamed. Lloyd concentrated all his energy on simply standing still against the shouts.

"Look at him, will you? Will you look at him?" The shortstop zipped the ball to first base, and Lloyd was out and it was over. For this time. Sweat streaked his temples, and his heart pounded just as much as if he had run.

"Spithead!" Shafer said, spitting and preparing for the next batter. His dark curls bobbed when he moved his head.

"Yeah. Spithead!" said Kirby, spitting into the dust.

Lloyd shuffled to the sidelines and stood at the end of the line. Spithead yourself, he thought. Shafer and Kirby thought they were such big stuff. So perfect. Well, he was bigger than both of them. Taller, and wider, too.

After the third out, Lloyd strolled toward right field. Halfway there, something pinched his foot. Ignoring their cries of "Hustle, hustle, hustle," he sat down and plucked the double knot from his shoelace. A ball came his way, and Kirby ran from center field to snag it.

"Saphead!" Kirby said.

"Little jerkhead," said Bobby, who had dropped back from second base in case he was needed. Lloyd dumped a pebble from his shoe, replaced the shoe, and left the lace to dangle.

"Big jerkhead, you mean," Marcia said, joining in from first base. "There's nothing little about Lloyd except his brain. Look, he's even too lazy to tie his shoes."

"He never ties them," Kirby said.

"Too fat to bend over is why," Bobby said.

Lloyd ignored their words, ignored the whole ball game as best he could. Soon he realized that the direction of the catcalls had changed, and he looked up. At bat was a new girl he'd barely noticed before. Her hair reminded him of spaghetti, the color of the sauce and as stringy as the noodles.

"Come on, swing!" Members of both teams shouted at her. "Swing at something." The girl was just as small for sixth grade as he was large. He dimly remembered that Mrs. Parker had introduced her to the class this morning. She'd just moved here from out of town somewhere. Now she stood with the bat on her shoulder and did not move it, no matter how many balls the pitcher threw. When Mrs. Parker's whistle blasted them from the field, the girl was still at bat.

"Wasted our whole recess. Little spithead," Shafer said. Everyone grumbled as they went to line up by the door.

"Spaghetti-head!" Lloyd snorted to the new girl as she passed him. He was shuffling along at his habitual slow pace, trying to be last.

"Lloyd, you come on up front so I can keep an eye on you," Mrs. Parker called to him. Hanging his head, he waggled his way to the front of the line, followed by the usual chorus of snickers. Mrs. Parker marched right alongside of him so there would be no trouble in line. Watching, watching, she was always watching. But, Lloyd thought, she watched with the wrong eye.

Since he was first in line, he was also first into the classroom and first at his desk in the first row. While Mrs. Parker stood in the doorway supervising the others, Bobby came down the aisle and flicked out a hand to jab Lloyd. As quick as a gator's tail, Lloyd lashed out. He grabbed Bobby's hand and twisted it sharply. While Lloyd was occupied with Bobby, Kirby frogged him on the shoulder, and Shafer snaked out with a speedy foot and kicked. Lloyd kicked back at Shafer, then Marcia yanked his hair and he yanked hers.

"All right, Lloyd, that's enough," Mrs. Parker said. He'd been at his desk, he guessed, less than fifteen seconds. Trouble didn't take long.

Lloyd sighed. He knew what Mrs. Parker meant just as he knew what team to be on when his name was not called. He didn't really mind moving to the discipline desk alongside of her own desk. Only there, safely away from his classmates, could he shut out the world and become himself.

The usual echo of giggles followed him as he carried his books and papers to the front of the room. Let them laugh, he thought. Sometimes, at least, he controlled what they laughed at. Every time he struck out, let them laugh. When he accidentally hit the ball and refused to run, let them laugh. If he ran, he knew they would laugh at his jouncing flesh, at his slow-molasses travel. Instead, he let them hee and haw and split their gizzards thinking he was too dumb or too dumbfounded to run. They didn't know everything. In fact, there was a lot they didn't know.

Sitting near the teacher, he slipped his hand into his pocket to thumb the olive shell. His eyes pressed through the cool greenness of the chalkboard. The color deepened and darkened and began to ripple until it became the sea and he was sitting by it, on the sand, just beyond the reach of the foamy surf. He was digging a moat and making the most fantastic sand castle ever, with drawbridges, turrets, and dungeons. In his mind, he put certain people in the dungeon—Shafer, Kirby, that dumb new girl and the rest of his classmates, Mrs. Parker, his mother. Guilt pinched him like crab claws. He puzzled over that last addition and then removed Mama from the dungeon.

He took the olive shell out of his pocket, set it on the desk, and gazed at it. He'd found it one rare day at the beach. Though the ocean was only eight miles away, across a flat causeway and five bridges, he'd been there only twice. Mama was afraid of the sea, afraid the moving water would capture him and take him away. She was always afraid that something or someone would take him away. But at least he had the olive shell, with all the colors of the seashore, and, though it was small, he could hold it to his ear and hear the sound of the sea.

"Lloyd, I don't see how you're going to pass this year if you don't pay attention to your work," Mrs. Parker said.

"Yes, ma'am," he said, smiling and nodding. He quickly covered the olive shell with his hand so she wouldn't see it and take it away from him. Passing was not the problem, he knew. He was in sixth grade, right where he was supposed to be, and not a year behind, like Bobby. No matter how many times he was absent, no matter how dumb they thought he was, he knew he was learning enough to pass.

As he bent his head to his work, his imagination plunged right through the paper, through the initial-scarred wood of the desk and back to the beach, back to wherever it was he wanted to be.

At three o'clock he began holding his breath and

watching the clock. At three-twelve he gathered his books and waited for three-fifteen. At the first peal of the bell, he jumped up and fled. Out of the classroom, out of the building, across the sidewalk and into Mama's car.

2

"HEY, BABY," MAMA SAID AS SHE LEANED OVER TO kiss him. "Your shoe is untied." She patted the seat between them, and Lloyd moved his foot onto the space. With nimble fingers she tied his shoe, then kissed her index and middle fingers and touched them to his cheek. For one more day he was safe.

At home they followed their springtime routine. She made him four toast and jellies and splashed a huge glass full of milk. While he was devouring his snack, she changed out of her shrimp-smelly uniform and into her shorts and shirt. Then she drove them the four blocks to the Rec Park.

"Hurry up, don't be so slow," her teammates heckled as Mama reached for her glove in the back seat of the car. As he hurried along beside her, Lloyd grinned. There was such friendliness in the teasing, not hatefulness as in the teasing of his classmates.

"Okay, everybody on the field," said Mama's friend, Geneva. She tossed a bat to Lloyd. Expertly he caught the bat and shouldered it as the women scattered for fielding practice. Crouching slightly, he stood ready as his mother prepared to pitch. She pulled her sandy brown hair into a ponytail to keep it off her face.

"Grounders first," Mama said. She fired a ball across home plate. He eyed it carefully and let it go by.

"Come on, Lloyd, baby. What are you waiting for?" The women chortled from the field, slapping hand and glove and chattering the machine-gun chatter, "Eh-eh-eh-eh-eh-swing."

On the second pitch he bounded one down the third-base line. On the third pitch he bounced one over the shortstop's head. Next he pulled up on the bat and bunted.

"I swear, all this practice with us is going to make you a star," Geneva said. She squatted behind him, catching. He ducked his head and grinned.

"Aw, I'm not that good," he said.

When they were ready for the fliers, he popped them short and fast and high and long. Geneva protested when one sailed over the fence.

"We're just practicing, Lloyd. Keep it inside the fence, will you?"

On the way home from practice Mama asked, as always, "What do you want for supper?"

"Spaghetti," he said. "With lots of garlic bread."

As soon as they walked in, she hurried to the kitchen to start dinner and he walked to the bathroom and began running his bath water. When he stepped into the tub, he sank back and let the water lap around him until it reached his shoulders and he was almost floating.

When Mama called, "Baby, you come on now," he began to wash, face first, without soap, then ears, neck, shoulders, arms, chest, bit by bit, until he finished with his feet. Afterward he wrapped himself in his cuddly blue velour robe and curled up in his green comfort chair and watched television. As the cooking progressed, he breathed deeply and watched Mama through the doorway as she set the kitchen table with matching things—place mats, plates, silverware, glasses.

"You're just trying to be highfalutin," Granny

would say, those times she came.

"I'm trying to be a good mother and have a decent household," Mama would answer. "Which is more than you ever thought I could do."

When he was a baby, Mama had told him, Granny and other people had tried to take him away from her. Mama had been only fourteen, and everyone thought she wouldn't know how to be a good mother. But she was. She was the best. She took care of him as though he were a prince, and he liked it. Fourteen. The thought chilled him beneath his blue robe. He was already twelve, and he didn't even know how to take care of himself. How had Mama managed? How had she learned?

Mama and Daddy had bundled him up and run away to keep Granny from taking him. He'd had two more fathers since then, but now it was just him and Mama. He liked it that way. And if place mats were highfalutin, then he liked being highfalutin.

"Mmmm," he said with gusto as she filled his plate to the edges. Steam rose like smoke from the red pool of sauce in the center of the spaghetti.

"How I love to see you eat," Mama said. "Some children are so finicky. But you are a pleasure to cook for." Lloyd smiled, his cheeks rising to crinkle his eyes.

"But I'm too fat, Mama," he said.

"Oh, go on. It's just your baby fat," she said. "You'll outgrow it, you'll see."

One of these days when he lost his baby fat and learned how to run fast, he'd sock the baseball clear over the schoolhouse roof. Then his classmates would know that he was highfalutin.

3

DURING SHARED STUDY TIME MRS. PARKER PAIRED
him with Marcia and sent them to the back table.
They had been studying the Alps and were supposed to quiz each other.

Lloyd hung his head and plodded to the back of
the room. All the others doubled up at their regular
desks for shared study. Whoever he was paired
with, though, had to join him at one of the tables.
There was no room for anyone else but Lloyd at a
regular school desk.

"Do you know the page?" Marcia asked, slapping

her book open loudly. He nodded and turned to the correct page. "What countries do the Alps go through?" she asked him. "Without looking at the book." He turned his book face down on the table.

"France, Italy, Switzerland, Germany, Austria, and Yugoslavia," he said. She had to check the book to be sure he was right. He was.

"What regions are the Alps divided into?" he asked her.

"Western, Central, and Eastern," Marcia said, and she stuck her tongue out at him. "What are the three highest peaks and what ranges are they in?"

He knew the answers. He especially liked geography and poring over maps. One day he would roam all over the world and be an adventurer, a skier, a mountain climber, and he would collect shells from beaches all over the world. One day. Now he said to Marcia, "Mont Blanc, Monte Rosa, and the Matterhorn, and they are all in the Pennines." He stuck his tongue out at her and turned it into a sloppy raspberry.

"What does the word 'alps' mean?" he asked.

"It's the name of the mountains, fathead. Even your brains are fat. They're too lazy to think up decent questions."

"No, the word 'alps' means a certain thing," he insisted.

Marcia raised her hand and waved it and started talking without waiting to be acknowledged. "Mrs. Parker, Lloyd did me a raspberry. Lloyd's being rude and asking dumb questions." The teacher was already heading toward them.

Lloyd said, "She stuck her tongue out at me first."

"What was your question, Lloyd?"

"I asked her what the word 'alps' meant." Marcia had raised her hand not because of the raspberry, he knew, but because she didn't know the answer to his question.

"It's just the name of the mountains, isn't it, Mrs. Parker?"

"Why don't you look it up?" While Mrs. Parker stood there, Marcia snatched a dictionary off the shelf.

"See, I told you," she said, poking her finger into the page. Marcia was a whiz with the dictionary. "The major mountain system of south central Europe," she read.

"I meant what the local people use the word for," he said.

"But that's not what you said," Marcia protested. "Besides, the Alps are just the Alps—isn't that right, Mrs. Parker?"

"Alpine peoples use the word 'alps' to designate

the high pastures above the tree line," Lloyd quoted from the geography book. "These meadows are used for grazing livestock."

"Well," Marcia said, "that's not even important, is it, Mrs. Parker?"

"It doesn't seem very significant," the teacher said.

"If it's not significant, why did they put it in the book?" he asked, but Mrs. Parker was already dismissing them and calling an end to the study period. Marcia clasped her book to her chest and huffed back to her desk. It would be significant to you if you lived there and had goats, he thought to her back. He pressed his lips together and waited until both Marcia and Mrs. Parker were in their places. Then he slowly returned to his desk.

At play period he shoved his hands in his pockets and swayed from side to side, scuffing his shoes in the dust. In one hand he cupped the olive shell. The earth at his feet was darker and finer than sand; it was gray-brown, one of the colors on the olive shell. He thought of himself sunning on the beaches of the world. He kept a half ear's attention for the next-to-last name so he'd know which team to be on. If he went with the wrong team, they'd really howl.

"Lloyd." Startled to hear his name, he looked up.

Shafer pointed to him with disgust and beckoned him over. To Lloyd's surprise, there was someone left standing.

"Come on, you," Kirby said to the scrawny red-haired girl.

"I have a name," she said haughtily. "It's Ancil."

A smile bobbled on Lloyd's lips. For once he wasn't chosen last. As he joined Shafer's team, he looked at the girl, held out one hand, and thrust a thumb downward.

"She sure is all kinds of ugly," someone said.

"Yeah," Lloyd said, chuckling to himself. "All kinds of ugly. Spaghetti-head."

This time her team got the hits and she came up to bat in the second inning. Without ever taking the bat from her small shoulders, she watched every ball go by. To Lloyd it seemed funnier and funnier, and he stood in right field chanting the rattling chant with the others.

"Eh-eh-eh-eh-eh-swing!" Even her own teammates began shouting, begging, "Swing! Swing! Swing!" If she kept this up, Lloyd's team would never get in again and he wouldn't have to come to bat.

"I'm waiting for a good ball," she said.

"You've had six thousand good balls," someone said.

"Give her a base," someone said. "Ball four. Base on balls."

"What does that mean?" the girl asked.

"You know we don't do base on balls," someone protested.

"But we'll be here all day."

"Come on," Kirby said. "Pitch." Four more balls went by and still she didn't swing. Then Mrs. Parker's whistle summoned them. Groans and curses shuttled through the air.

"It's all those freckles," someone said. "They go clear across her face and cover her eyes. She can't even see the ball. That's why she doesn't swing."

"Yeah," Lloyd said loudly, feeling jaunty. "It's all those freckles. Her spaghetti hair splatters all over her face. She's all kinds of ugly." He stooped to pluck at a disappearing sock. Then he reached out and grabbed at her small ankle as she passed by. With a hip and a hop, she managed to keep from falling, but he was pleased with himself just the same. He swaggered as he moved to the head of the line, where Mrs. Parker had directed him.

At his desk he sat, again poised over his sock as though ready to pull it up. When Shafer flexed a leg to bop Lloyd in the side of the head with his knee, Lloyd was ready. As Shafer's knee came forward,

Lloyd grabbed it and upended Shafer onto the floor.

"Lloyd!" Mrs. Parker stood with her arms crossed.

"I wished you'd watch, really watch," Lloyd said bitterly as he tromped to the discipline desk. "You never see what they do."

"I see quite enough, thank you," she said. It was as useless, he knew, as trying to explain that Marcia had stuck out her tongue first. "And I hear quite enough, too," Mrs. Parker said. "I saw you try to trip Ancil, and I heard what you said to her, too."

See, see. Hear, hear, he thought. What kind of filters did she have on her eyes and ears to see and hear only what *he* did or said and not the others?

At the discipline desk he leaned over and tugged at his sock. It would not come up. He plucked at the double-tied shoelace, untied it, pulled up his sock and left the lace dangling. Then he stared at the chalkboard and let the green become the magnificent evergreens of the Alps. The chalk marks were snow. He would wear wide suspenders, short pants, and one of those pointed hats with a feather. He would tend goats above the tree line, in the Alps, and learn to yodel. From the top of Mont Blanc he would schuss down into the heart of Geneva. Geneva, the city in Switzerland. Geneva, his mother's friend. He liked them both. Someday he would be a world-famous explorer and shell collector, and people would come up to him and say, "Didn't you used to go to Sidney Lanier Elementary School in Hanover, Georgia?" And he would say, "I've lived in Europe all my life." Someday.

As he left class, they teased him some more.

"Stupidhead's too fat to bend over to tie his shoes."

"You mean too lazy."

"Too fat and too lazy."

He didn't bother to look back. He was on his downward run, down the hall, down the stairs, out and away. In the car Mama tied his shoe.

4

ON WEEKEND MORNINGS MAMA LET LLOYD SLEEP. Or if they had to go somewhere, she padded quietly into his room and soothed him awake. But on school days, no matter how gentle she was, Lloyd couldn't be soothed.

"Good morning, baby. Time to get up." Her fingers fluttered through his hair.

"Do I have to?" he asked, hunching down into the bed.

"Yes, baby, you have to. You get on up and I'll fix breakfast." She kissed him lightly on the forehead.

Her pink furry slippers whispered, "Hush, hush, hush," as they moved across the floor. Dangling one arm over the side of the bed, he reached for the olive shell. Every night at bedtime he tucked it between the mattress and the box spring. With the shell in his hands, he tried to rub away the dread of school. But not even the olive shell could chase away his misery.

The salt-pork smell of bacon curled through the air. He stared out the window through the gauze of tree leaves and decided that he would not get out of bed.

"Okay, baby. Breakfast is ready," Mama called. It was easy to hear her in the small house. There was only the one bedroom that she let him have for his own privacy. She slept on the sofa bed in the living room. If he got up, he knew he would see the sofa already back in place. And she would be dressed in her white uniform and made up with lipstick and eye shadow. Once more he shifted his position and turned his face to the wall so he wouldn't see her when she came so pretty into the room.

"Hey, baby, come on," she said. If he turned to look, he knew she would be standing in the doorway as in the middle of a picture frame. To anchor himself, he gripped the edge of the sheet.

"Lloyd, come on now." Her voice was peppered

with irritation, and he hated it. Peace. All he wanted was peace.

"Can't she come here?" he said into his pillow.

"Who? Can't who come here?"

"The teacher." Why should he go somewhere that caused him such distress?

"Lloyd Albert, we've been through this sixty-eleven times. You know I don't have time for this." She came over to the bed now, crunched her fingers into his shoulder, and rolled him onto his back. Still, he kept the sheet clutched in his fists. "Lloyd, come on. Get up!" She wrenched the sheet from his hands. There were spikes in the tone of her voice. "Lloyd, if you miss any more school, they'll take you away from me."

Though he had heard it all his life, the threat pierced him anew. If she didn't take good care of him, they would take him away from her. If he acted too sulky or if he refused to go to school, they would take him away from her. He both loved and hated her. Didn't she know he would do almost anything to please her? But school. School stripped him of himself until he was painfully bare.

With one motion she swung his legs to the edge of the bed, gripped his shoulder, and sat him up. He pitched over the other way. She had taken a first-aid course and knew how to move a person who was unconscious. How had he forgotten that? He was the one she had practiced on. Still, he outweighed her by fifty pounds. He knew she would not roll him off the bed and drag him to the car, then shove him out limp in front of the school. People would see then and think she was not a good mother.

"I'm telling you," she said once more. "They'll make you leave and go someplace where you'd still have to go to school."

He was now headfirst at the foot of the bed, and he regathered the sheet into his hands. The sheet and the olive shell were his shields against her words. Her words were merely threats. No one could really take him away. No one could really make him go to school.

"Lloyd, you know my time schedule. You know I have to go now." He knew. She had power, but he had power, too. He had the power to lie like a lump so that all her pushing, pulling, tugging, and shoving could not budge him.

She left with the silent steps of rubber-soled shoes. He held his breath and stayed still. The front door closed. The car chugged to a start. Was she really leaving? The temptation to run to the front window nearly overcame him. But perhaps she was thinking he would run to the window. Perhaps she was lurking, waiting to pounce. With the olive shell in his hand, he clung to the sheet and pressed his body into the mattress.

After enough time had passed, he tiptoed to the window. The car was not in the driveway. She was gone. She was really gone. The silence of the house surrounded him like a safe, sunny cloud, soft and light and quiet. He relaxed and let the house enfold him.

On stay-home days he usually turned on the television. The game shows and soap operas carried him out of himself more surely than the chalkboard. From a game show he had learned that the highest-ranking suit of cards in the game of bridge was spades. And that the North Star and the polestar were the same, and its name was Polaris, and it was the star at the end of the handle of the Little Dipper.

Today, however, he did not turn on the television. Somehow today was different. Usually he pretended to be sick in order to stay home. He whined and wheedled and maneuvered. But today he had made a deliberate decision: *I will not go to school.*

Sitting in his green comfort chair, he curled his arms around his knees and listened to the wonderful emptiness of the house. When he breathed, he heard his own breath. In. Out. In. Out.

The remnant odor of bacon broke his concentration on breathing. His stomach signaled *hungry-hungry-hungry.* Had she left his breakfast for him? If not, he might have to eat lunch early. He sauntered into the kitchen. There was nothing on the stove or in the oven. The frying pan was clean and upside down in the dish drainer. Maybe she had put his breakfast in the refrigerator, though he wrinkled his face at the thought of cold eggs and grits.

Even opening the refrigerator door sounded noisy in the quiet house. There was no plate of eggs, grits, and bacon. What had she done with it? It was unlike her to throw anything away. Staring into the white enamel interior of the refrigerator, he realized that he did not see his lunch plate, either. When he stayed home, she always fixed him three or four different kinds of sandwiches, wrapped and stacked on a plate. And she filled his milkshake-size glass with milk.

For a moment he was hollow with abandonment. So? He'd have to wait until she came home. If he tried to pour the milk, he'd spill it and make a mess and she'd be angry.

Back in the green comfort chair, he flicked on the television with the remote control switch. Keeping his finger on the button, he circled the channels, then stopped at a game show. Contestants were trying to win fantastic amounts of money by matching sequences of numbers. He wished he could be on a show like that. If he had lots of money, Mama wouldn't have to work at the shrimp plant and come home all smelly. He would buy them a house by the ocean where there was no school. And he would learn to swim so well that she would lose her fear of the sea.

5

DURING COMMERCIALS, WHEN FOOD WAS ADVER-
tised, his stomach threatened to charge into the
television set. Why hadn't Mama fixed him some
food?

"Be quiet," he told his stomach, but it signaled
hungry-hungry-hungry like a programmed robot.
"Okay, okay," he said after a while, and he took his
stomach to the kitchen.

What could he fix? He looked around the kitchen.
The toaster gleamed silver from the counter top.
Toast shouldn't be too hard. He undid the yellow

plastic twist-tie from the bread package and put a slice of bread in each of the toaster slots. They stayed there. Cautiously, hoping he wouldn't shock himself, he pressed the handle. The bread went down as if it were in an elevator, and he smiled with satisfaction. He removed the margarine from the refrigerator and picked open the ends of the wrapper. Knife in hand, he stood waiting for the toast to pop up.

But if it didn't?

The toast would burn.

He tried to push up the handle, but it resisted his pressure. My toast will burn, he thought, frantic now. Gripping the handle firmly with both hands, he pushed it up. The bread rose, steaming hot, but still white. Laughing at himself, he shoved the handle back down. In a few seconds it popped up again, the bread still white. Four times he pushed the handle down, and four times it popped back up.

"I've broken the toaster!" he howled out loud. "Mama will kill me." Taking the bread from the slots, he burned his hands and let go of the bread. One slice landed on the counter, the other on the floor. He picked up the slice from the floor and took it to the kitchen door. Opening the door, he flung the bread into the side yard.

"Here, Kitty-kitty. Here, Kitty-kitty," he called.

Maybe this time she would come to him. He sat on the steps to watch for her, but instead of Kitty-kitty, one of the cocky boat-tailed grackles swooped down.

"No!" he shouted, running toward the glossy crow-sized bird. In fact, he used to think they were crows until Mama had informed him otherwise. "No! That's for Kitty-kitty." The bird flew in retreat, and Lloyd picked up the bread and tore it into bits. Perhaps if he made a trail of crumbs from the edge of the yard to the steps, he could entice the cat to come.

"I'm sorry it's not fish," he said aloud to the striped cat, wherever she was. If he sat very still and wished very hard, he thought she might appear and nibble her way along the bread-crumb path.

But as soon as he sat back on the steps, he was sorry he had spread the bread across the yard. The grackle kept trying to land and Lloyd charged around the yard, waving his arms. The bird darted to the far side of the yard and captured a crumb before Lloyd moved close enough to chase it away.

"You're a smart little devil, aren't you?" Lloyd said. He watched the bird take the crumb to a safe distance and lift its head to let the morsel drop into its throat. The feathers on the bird, though black, contained green and pink and purple like the rainbow in a puddle of oil. "Okay, you might as well have it," he said, and he sat back on the steps, thinking sadly of Kitty-kitty.

He didn't know who the cat belonged to. He thought she was a stray. She looked scrawny and lonesome, but when he and Mama put scraps out for her, she wouldn't let them get close. Thinking about the cat, he forgot the bird until it had nibbled its way as close as he had intended the cat to come.

Rocking from side to side, from one foot to the other, as Lloyd himself did when whiling away the time on the ball field, the bird hopped one step closer. There were three crumbs left. Lloyd held his breath and sat without moving. The bird hopped forward, grabbed the third crumb, and fluttered back, gulping the crumb and making a chuckling sound in its throat. With a swaggering strut it moved in again, swiftly snatched the second-to-last crumb, and dropped back to swallow it. After much throat chuckling and sashaying back and forth, the grackle flew three feet in the air and dive-bombed the last crumb right at the tip of Lloyd's shoe.

Lloyd sat enchanted as the bird strutted down the line where the bread had been, dusting its beak against the ground for any last crumbs. Lloyd thought of the other slice of bread on the kitchen counter, but he knew that if he moved the spell would be broken. When the bird finally flew away, Lloyd returned to the kitchen.

The other slice of bread was cold now, and he put it back in the toaster and pushed the handle down. He peered into the slot and felt the heat on his face as he tried to watch the bread toasting. When he popped the handle up and lifted the bread out, it was golden-brown.

Smiling, he sliced a chunk of margarine and tried to spread it on the hot toast, but the yellow cube simply moved around ahead of the knife. When he pressed it, to force it to spread, it gouged holes in the bread. Maddened by the quick turn of success into failure, he stuffed the toast into his mouth, lump of margarine and all.

Maybe, he thought, he would eat soup. Cold, of course. He would never try to use the stove. Mama said that more accidents happened in the kitchen than in any other room of the house. It was because of the stove and all the sharp knives. He took a can of chicken noodle soup from the cabinet and reached for the can opener. Somehow Mama attached the thing to a can and went twist-twist-twist. So easy. So hard. The can opener was a metal puzzle.

He decided to risk the milk. He poured raisin bran into a bowl, gripped the gallon jug, and tipped it toward the bowl. A cascade of milk splatted into the center of the bowl, and bran flakes and milk slopped onto the counter. He sopped up the spilled milk with a dishcloth, ooky in his hand, and raked the stray flakes into the sink. The too-dry cereal did not fill his stomach. His belly cried all afternoon as he thought about food and waited for Mama to come home and fix his snack.

As always, she came in a rush and whooshed straight into the kitchen. In quick one-two-three motions she popped bread into the toaster, set margarine on the counter, and slivered it into thin slices. She zipped to the bathroom, removed her fish-smelly uniform, returned to the kitchen in her slip, caught the toast slices as they popped up, and dabbed them with thin pats of margarine. So, he thought, it does pop up by itself.

She put two more pieces of bread in the toaster, skimmed the knife across the hot toast, and spread the margarine smoothly. The razor-thin slices melted easily onto the hot toast. He smiled, pleased with his observations. He watched as she finished buttering, slid strawberry jam over the top, splashed a huge glass of milk, and set everything on the table.

"Thanks, Mama. I'm starved," he said. "Can I have more?"

With swift, sure movements she began the process again. Slowly he became aware that she had not kissed him hello and she had not said a word.

Was she still mad about this morning? She plopped four more pieces of toast in front of him and refilled his milk glass. Then she darted to the bathroom, reappeared in shorts and shirt, and headed for the door. Quickly he gathered the rest of the jelly toast in one hand and started after her.

"No!" she said, turning on him, pointing her index finger at him. "You stay here." Her words were like bullets, and he was shot through.

"By myself?" he said.

"You stayed by yourself all day," she said.

"But that's different. This is practice time."

The door slammed and her sneakered feet thonked softly across the yard to the car. He stood as still as if she had sprayed him with Freezone, that stuff she put on his foot to clip away a wart. The house was not a sanctuary now—it was a dark dungeon.

6

THE SOUND OF A CAR IN THE DRIVEWAY LIFTED
his spirits. She had changed her mind and come
back for him. He leaped for the door, ready to fly
out and not waste precious practice time. With the
front door flung back and his hand at the center bar
of the screen door, he stopped cold. It was not
Mama's car. A tall man with wavy blond hair got
out. It was Mr. Duggan, who had something to do
with school. Mr. Duggan had come before to talk to
Mama about Lloyd's absences. Lloyd started to shut
the door, but the man had already spotted him.

"Hello, Lloyd," Mr. Duggan said, stepping onto the porch, reaching for the door handle. "May I come in?"

Lloyd quickly latched the hook on the screen door. "Mama says for me not to let strangers in," he said.

Mr. Duggan laughed. "Well, I'm hardly a stranger. In fact, it seems I see more and more of you. But your mother has taught you a good rule, and I can talk quite well from here. Is your mother home?"

He watched Mr. Duggan look through the crosshatching of the screen to examine the room. Lloyd stared at the wire until Mr. Duggan's face was blocked off in tiny squares like a needlepoint picture. You are a stranger, Lloyd thought, whether you think so or not.

"If she was here, you'd see her car in the driveway," he said. Immediately he was annoyed with himself. He had given Mr. Duggan a valuable clue. Whenever the car was in the driveway, Mr. Duggan would know Mama was home.

"Well, it's just as well she's not here," Mr. Duggan said. "This is really between you and me, anyway, isn't it?"

Lloyd pressed his finger onto the latch to be sure it stayed hooked.

"I think you're old enough for me to be perfectly

straight with, aren't you?" Mr. Duggan asked. "You know we have a law that requires boys and girls to go to school."

Sure, sure, Lloyd thought. They'd explained that to him, all about how some children used to be kept out of school to do farm work or factory work or to take care of younger brothers and sisters. Well, he didn't work and he didn't have brothers or sisters and he didn't need a dumb old law to be sure he got his education. He could study by himself at home.

"The absolute limit of school days to miss in one school year is forty-five," Mr. Duggan said. "Do you have any idea how many days you've missed already?"

Lloyd's eyes wandered around the yard and examined the bare limbs of the enormous oak that had been struck by lightning last year. No leaves. The lightning had killed it, and the landlord was going to have it removed. He knew he must be right at the limit of days for them to be so concerned about it.

"Forty-four?" Lloyd said, because Mr. Duggan was waiting for him to guess.

"Sixty-four," Mr. Duggan said. "You are way over the limit. The only reason something hasn't been done is that I've been plugging for you. I hear from your teacher that you are a bully and a troublemaker, but I just don't believe that. I really wish I could help you."

You could help by leaving me alone, Lloyd thought. He spotted Kitty-kitty over by the dead tree and knew if he went out right now she would come to him, but he couldn't open the door because of Mr. Duggan.

"I'll tell Mama you came by," Lloyd said, trying to end the encounter.

"No, you don't have to do that. I don't think we should put the responsibility on your mother, Lloyd. I think you are old enough to start being responsible for yourself."

Right, Lloyd thought. He thought of this morning with Mama, not pretending to be sick but being responsible for himself and making his own decision to stay home. He remembered how powerful he had felt. And he had some power now, too.

"I have to go now," he said to Mr. Duggan, and he smiled politely and closed the door right in the man's face. He scampered to his bedroom and sat on the bed.

Alternating between anger at Mr. Duggan and delight in his own cleverness, he forgot to listen for the sound of the car. As with Mama this morning, he didn't know if Mr. Duggan had gone away or was lurking somewhere. But what did it matter? Lloyd was locked securely inside, and Mr. Duggan didn't have a key.

After a while Lloyd moseyed back to the living-room window and looked out. No car. Kitty-kitty was gone, too. He unlocked the door and went out.

"Kitty-kitty. Here, Kitty-kitty." He walked around the tree and around the yard, but the striped cat did not appear.

"What do you want to eat?" Mama asked when she came home.

Lloyd looked at her warily. "Country fried steak, mashed potatoes, gravy, green beans, and ice cream for dessert," he said as though it were all one word. Had Mr. Duggan gone to the ball field and talked to Mama in spite of saying it was between the two of them?

He ran the bath water and sat soaking while Mama started dinner. His fingers and toes wrinkled as he waited for her to call out to him.

Finally she knocked on the door and said, "Dinner's ready."

"Already?" he asked, which was not what he meant. What he meant was why hadn't she called him in time for him to watch TV before dinner, like always?

She dished food onto his plate without chattering

as she usually did. He wanted her to say they had missed him, had needed him for fielding practice.

"How did practice go?" he asked.

"Okay," she said without adding to it. Mr. Duggan must have talked to her. It wasn't like her to stay mad so long.

But at bedtime he was relieved that she hugged him and kissed him and tucked him in the same as ever.

7

AT THE REC PARK THE NEXT DAY SOME OF THE women were running around the field.

"What are they doing?" Lloyd asked.

"Running laps, baby. We started that yesterday," Mama said, and she trotted off and left him.

"Come on, run with us!" Geneva called. Lloyd shook his head. They thought he was great, the way he could hit a ball. If they saw how slow he was when he ran, they would change their minds.

"Come on, run," Geneva said as she came around the field, finishing her first lap.

"I'm too slow," he mumbled.

"Aw, come on. Everyone is slow at first," she said, but she galloped off without him.

For grounding practice, Mama often pitched easy balls, to be sure the fielders got a lot of practice. Sometimes, though, she fired her best, and her best was the best in the league.

"The harder they come, the harder they go!" Geneva yelled as Mama whizzed one toward him. He swung hard, connecting with the ball in a satisfying sharp crack.

"Second base," he shouted. He often knew where the ball would go. It was as though his brain were a computer and could figure out the speed and angle of the approaching ball as well as the speed and angle of the swinging bat. The ball bounded toward second base so fast that it whisked past the baseman and onto center field.

"Good one, Lloyd!"

"Attaway, Lloyd, baby!" Their encouragement bounded back from the field.

When the team was ready for batting practice, he handed over the bat and turned toward the third-base bench. To his surprise, Kirby, from school, was sitting on the bench and staring at him. Jaw knotted, brain trying to think up snappy answers for what he knew would be coming from Kirby's smart-aleck mouth, Lloyd kept on walking. Without acknowledging Kirby, he sat on the opposite end of the bench.

"I don't believe it," Kirby said. "How come you don't hit like that at school?" Lloyd kept his mouth shut while he slid his hand into his pocket to touch the olive shell. "You're really terrific, do you know that?"

Had Kirby really said he was terrific? Terrific? The look and the word mellowed the space between them.

"You really think so?" Lloyd asked.

"I don't understand it. I just don't understand it," Kirby said. "If I could hit like that, I'd want everyone in the world to know it." Lloyd made no further comment, and Kirby got up. "I'm going to pick you for my team Monday. I mean, without waiting for last." Kirby hopped on a green-and-black spider bike and sped away.

Joy and sorrow were mixed within Lloyd, and his head sank between his shoulders. He was glad that someone knew that he could really clout the ball. But he didn't want Kirby to choose him for a team. He didn't want the people at school to know his private business. Already he felt exposed.

The weekend was not long enough, and on Monday morning he was sick, really sick. Sick with the thought of facing everyone at school after Kirby's telling mouth.

"Lloyd, I mean it, you have to get up," Mama said, leaning over him, pulling at the sheet.

In a very small voice he said, "I'm sick, Mama. I really am sick." He imagined how it would be, with Kirby telling everyone how Lloyd could hit that ball. Just thinking about it made him feel as if all his clothes had been stripped away and he were standing in the school yard in his birthday suit.

Mama sighed with exasperation. "All right, Lloyd," she said. "I'll fix your lunch."

He stayed in bed until she was gone, and even then he didn't get up for a while. The house didn't surround him with magnificent silence this time. The stillness seemed threatening. The quiet was a defeat. Why did all the other kids seem to get along okay?

Finally, his ever-controlling stomach forced him up. As he passed through the living room, he stopped and stared. Mama had left the sofa bed out with the rumpled covers in a heap. If she had ever left it undone before, sprawling like a giant snail out of its shell, he couldn't remember. Stretched out across half the living room, the opened sofa bed seemed to rebuke him. When he reached out to fold it back inside itself, it would not go. He pulled the covers off and threw them to the floor. Then he pushed the frame up, then down, and it slid into place. But the pile of covers was still in the middle of the floor—the blanket, the sheets, and the pillow. He sank into them and began to cry, wailing like thunder. He remembered his mother talking with disapproval about one of his aunts who bellowed when she cried. The thought made him bellow more.

His stomach growled. Food, like Mama's car after school, was always a comfort. In the refrigerator was a huge glass of milk. Stacked like a skyscraper were four sandwiches on one plate. He peeled off the plastic wrap and lifted the corner of each sandwich to peek at the contents. There was tuna, bologna, ham, and salami. Mama knew he didn't like four sandwiches all alike. Thinking of her loving thoughtfulness and his own uncooperative hatefulness almost made him cry again.

Just for himself, he set a place mat on the table. Would she be pleased if she knew? As he ate, he stared out the kitchen window. Here and there a few determined scraggles of grass flourished. Would she be pleased to have a pretty yard? Pouring his imagination through the glass, he saw a thick green lawn. A border of pansy faces looked back at him.

Across the border of imagined pansies rolled a very real truck—right into the yard. It had a ladder-bucket rig across the back. Telephone truck? Georgia Power truck? Then a dump truck parked at the curb. A man walked toward the house and rang the doorbell.

"Yes?" Lloyd said from behind the closed door. Mama always said you couldn't be too careful.

"We're fixing to start taking down this dead tree," the man said. "Be sure to stay over on the driveway side and be real careful."

"Yes, sir," Lloyd said.

Back in the kitchen, he stood at the window eating his sandwiches and watching the men put on hard hats. One man climbed into the bucket rig. With a *zzz-zzz* sound, a steel arm raised the bucket among the tree limbs, and with some more *zzz-zzzing*, the man in the bucket began snipping the ends of the limbs. On the ground the men hauled the fallen branches to the back of the dump truck.

All afternoon he watched as the tree was nipped back, bit by bit. In between watching, he worked to fold the covers from the sofa bed. The sheets, however, were flimsy and resisted his efforts. Each time he smoothed out one part it furrowed in another.

"Come on now," he said aloud. The men were

taking down the tree more easily than he could fold the sheets. Of course, they had equipment. What he needed was a sheet-folding machine. Finally he just rolled the sheets around his arms, dumped them on his bed, and went back to watching the men.

8

HE WAS STILL AT THE WINDOW, WATCHING
every limb as it was amputated from the tree, when
Mama came home. He ran outside to greet her.

"So they're taking the tree down," she said. "It's
kind of sad."

He looked at her, surprised that she should know
the sadness. As they reached the front door,
another car pulled into the driveway. Lloyd turned
his head, then stiffened. It was that Mr. Duggan
person.

"You're trying to scare me," he said to Mama, and

he hurriedly pulled open the screen door. But she was rushing inside with him and she put one arm around him in a tight grip. Then he noticed that her lips were pressed into a thin white line. They stood there together, twin fortresses against the intruder.

"Hello, Lloyd. Hello, Mrs. Albert," Mr. Duggan said, all friendly-like as he stood on their narrow porch. Lloyd wanted to spit. "I think we have something to talk about, don't you?"

Mama made no move to open the door.

"I think we can manage this better if we all sit down and try to relax," Mr. Duggan said.

Mama reached out to push the door open. Lloyd quickly stretched his arm out to restrain her, but it was too late. Mr. Duggan was coming in. Mama's arm was still around Lloyd and, like a couple dancing, they stepped back together, step-back-step, retreating into their own living room. Mama noticed the closed-up sofa and glanced at Lloyd in acknowledgment.

"You know I don't like doing this," Mr. Duggan said. "But it's part of my job." Mr. Duggan sat perched on the edge of Lloyd's green comfort chair, knees apart, forearms resting on his knees. Lloyd wished the chair were a robot chair so that, on command, it would swallow Mr. Duggan or send him sailing to the stars. He pictured Mr. Duggan turning end over end, going farther and farther away. A-w-a-a-ay.

"You know the law requires children to attend school until they are sixteen."

Lloyd sat on the sofa beside Mama, rocking back and forth and concentrating on making Mr. Duggan invisible. Mama put a hand on his back to still his motion.

Mr. Duggan's voice droned on. "You know what happens when people don't obey the law, don't you?"

This, now, was a new twist. A new threat. Terror seeped into Lloyd's veins. Would they take him to jail? He could not even reach into his pocket for the olive shell.

"No, we don't go around putting twelve-year-old boys in jail, if that's what you're thinking. However, we sometimes take them to a special home where they have to attend school."

"I try to make him go," Mama said, "but he's sick a lot." Her hand was still on his back, and her fingers pressed hard against his spine, bone on bone. "He hates it so. He likes to learn things, so it's not that he doesn't like the work." She trailed off into silence.

"Yes, I understand that. I'd like you to tell me about it, Lloyd. Why do you hate it so?" Mr. Duggan asked. "What's so bad about it?"

Words rumbled around in Lloyd's throat and circled his mouth. He wanted to remain silent, but he could feel Mama's desperation traveling through him from her fingertips.

"They don't like me," he muttered.

"Why don't they like you?" The man's voice was soft and without challenge. Mr. Duggan hadn't told Mama about coming here and having the door shut in his face.

On the wall was a picture Mama bought at Woolworth's. It was a picture of woods and a stream. Lloyd gazed past Mr. Duggan's shoulder and walked into the woods.

" 'Cause I'm fat and I can't run fast," he said from the distance, back in the shelter of trees that were still full of leaves and limbs. Bareness—that's why he suffered along with the tree in the yard, the sense of being stripped bare by his classmates and their yammering mouths.

"Not everybody can run fast. Long-legged as I am, I can't run fast," Mr. Duggan said. "And I'll bet there are other things you do really well. Can you think of some?"

A grin trickled to Lloyd's lips. "I can hit a ball," he said. "Except they don't know it."

"Why don't they know it? Don't you play ball at school?"

Lloyd's grin broadened. "Yes, sir. We play. But I just swing at the first three balls and make a strikeout."

"Lloyd! Why would you do that?" Mama said in surprise. "He's a good ball player. He practices with my softball team, and he bats for us to have fielding practice. He's really good."

"What makes them madder than anything is when I accidentally hit the ball and then don't run to base. I just stand there like I'm so surprised I hit it that I can't think to run."

"Lloyd!" Mama stared at him in disbelief.

"But if you can hit it, why don't you run?" Mr. Duggan asked. "You might even make a homer."

"I could," he said.

"He certainly could," Mama added.

"Then why don't you?"

Lloyd saw all the taunting faces, heard the shouts of disapproval. "Because they laugh at me. Besides, I *like* to make them mad."

"Oh. I understand," Mr. Duggan said, nodding, mouth and eyes all solemn. "I think we all feel that way sometimes. When someone hurts our feelings, we want to do something to get back at them."

Lloyd nodded, surprised at the understanding.

"In fact, I used to tease my brother just to upset him because he was older and smarter and stronger."

"What did you do?" Lloyd asked.

"Lloyd!" Mama said as though it were an impolite question.

"Well, he said it," Lloyd answered, wiggling away from the iron pressure of her fingers.

"It's funny, in a way, because it was a silly thing that upset him. He had a crooked nose, very slightly crooked, because it had been broken once. It wasn't even noticeable, really, but he thought it was terribly crooked. So I called him 'rhinoceros nose' one day, and it made him furious."

"Rhinoceros nose?" Lloyd giggled, imagining a boy with a snout as big as a rhinoceros's.

"And since it was so effective, I kept calling him that," Mr. Duggan said. "That's how it is with you, I guess. Not hitting the ball is effective."

"Yeah," Lloyd said. But he didn't tell Mr. Duggan that hitting the ball was his own special secret for his own special pleasure. Showing his skill to those oafs would spoil it. Why should he reveal his finest self to them? But he did promise to go to school. One more day's absence and they'd take him away. Mr. Duggan convinced him of that.

Later, at the ball field, Kirby stood astride the green-and-black spider bike, waiting for Lloyd. Lloyd ran past him and picked up the bat, tossed a ball in the air, and whacked it. Mama, taking a lap around the outfield, scooped it up and pitched it back, and Lloyd kept tossing and hitting until the women finished laps and were ready for fielding practice. When they were ready for batting practice, Lloyd walked out to right center field to avoid Kirby. Kirby watched for a while longer, then pedaled away.

In bed that night Lloyd put his hand behind his head and stared into the darkness. The house seemed deserted, even though he knew Mama was bedded down in the living room. The ghost of the limbless tree was infecting the house. The tree was empty, the house was empty, he was empty.

He thought of Mama, alone in that broad bed which she had, at different times, shared with his two stepfathers. On those mornings she hadn't been so quick to get up to fix breakfast, but had come more slowly awake, cuddling and snuggling with whichever daddy was with her then. He hadn't liked it, having an intruder in the house, even though he'd had some good times, too. It was his third father, as a matter of fact, who had taken them to the beach twice. It was his third father, he recalled, who had known the name of the olive shell. He reached beneath the mattress and rubbed his thumb along the cool smooth surface of the shell.

9

"WELL, IF IT ISN'T *LORD ALBERT* COMING TO school for a change," Bobby said as Lloyd shoved open the heavy door. Bobby was on hall patrol. He was supposed to keep students from fighting or running in the hall.

"Of course he's here," said Marcia, who was passing by. "He was absent yesterday. He comes every other day, haven't you figured that out yet?"

Pretending to be deaf and blind, Lloyd walked on and tromped up the stairs. As soon as he was in the classroom, Mrs. Parker took up the charge.

"Well, good morning, Lloyd. I'm glad you saw fit to join us for a change."

Lloyd glared at her. He was at school for only one reason. That didn't mean he had to like it. He decided he would be a turtle. Inside his mind, he would carve himself a thick shell and keep himself safely inside.

"Lloyd, when you are absent, we don't seem to have all these constant problems in the classroom." Mrs. Parker had moved over to his desk to speak to him privately, but those nearby could certainly hear. "When you are at your desk, I want you to keep your feet clamped together. And when you're not using your hands for schoolwork, keep them folded together on top of the desk where I can see them at all times." She paused for emphasis. "I warn you, I will be watching."

Watching, watching, she was always watching. If he stayed inside his shell, he would not even notice her watching. He would not notice when his classmates passed his desk and poked at him. They could not reach him inside his shell.

During the morning as they passed back and forth to the pencil sharpener, Shafer and Marcia landed quick blows. Stolid as a turtle, Lloyd did not move. He did not even blink.

"What's wrong with Lloyd?" Marcia whispered so

he could hear. "He must be dead. He's sitting right there at his desk, dead."

"Yeah, he'll start to stink soon," Bobby said.

"What do you mean? He already stinks."

On the school grounds, when they started choosing teams, he stared at his shoes. They would call the names down to the end, then not even call his name. Unless they chose *her* last, like the other day. He looked at her. She had a tiny runt face, as if her head had been pinched. And that awful hair, the color of spaghetti sauce. What was her name? Ancil? What kind of name was that?

When half the teams were chosen, he heard his own name. He looked up with a start. Kirby was motioning him over.

"He can hit," Kirby said to the others. "He can really hit. I saw him do it at the Rec Park."

"Yeah, I'll bet."

"Lucky fluke."

"Kirby's gone soft in the head."

Lloyd slowly moved over to join Kirby's team. When they got down to the last, they didn't call Ancil's name.

"No fair, no fair," some of the team members shouted. "It's not fair to have both Lloyd and her on the same team." Ancil just stood there.

"You, stupid," Lloyd said. "You're on this team."

"They didn't call my name."

"They don't call the names of spaghetti-heads," he said. Not wanting to be left with her, for once he hustled himself to the field.

"Come on, hit it now," Kirby said when Lloyd came up to bat. "He can really hit that ball. You should see! Come on, Lloyd, baby, give it a stroke." Kirby clapped his hands and shouted encouragement just like Geneva and Mama.

Lloyd stood ready, bat cocked just off his shoulder. At the first pitch he swung and missed.

"Don't swing at everything," his team members howled.

"Come on, Lloyd, baby. Show them you can do it!" Kirby yelled.

"Eh-eh-eh-eh-eh-swing," the other team chanted. And Lloyd swung the second time, and then he swung the third time and struck out. He moved to the end of the line. Kirby kicked the dirt and muttered under his breath.

Ancil came up to bat last and took up the rest of their play period watching every ball go by without swinging at all.

"Put the two of them in a mixer and you might come out with one normal-sized, halfway-decent ballplayer," Bobby said.

"They'd come out fat, dumb, and slow with red hair and freckles!" said Shafer.

"Look. Even Lloyd's shoes are fat. They've eaten his socks again," said Marcia. Before he could remember to be an unresponding turtle, he reached down and tugged at his socks.

But in class he turtled at his desk, unmoving, and let them pummel him as they passed. Kirby, he noticed, walked by without poking him.

"Shafer! Marcia! Boys and girls!" Mrs. Parker's voice snapped the classroom to silence. "Class, I'm ashamed of you. Lloyd, I may have an apology to make to you. I was watching, boys and girls. I was watching to keep Lloyd from hitting you as you passed his desk. And do you know what I saw? Lloyd didn't so much as move, and at least five of you hit him as you went by."

Lloyd chewed on the inside of his mouth. At last she had seen with her right eye. Some of his classmates looked at him, and he ducked his head.

"It's too bad I don't have five discipline desks," Mrs. Parker said. "But come on up, Shafer. We'll start with you." The classroom snickers that usually followed Lloyd to the discipline desk now accompanied Shafer.

On the way to wash his hands before lunch, Lloyd

swaggered down the hall. When he passed Ancil, he said, "Girl, you need to wash your face with Clorox to get rid of all those spots. And put some on your hair, too." He laughed, gloated and gloried at his own words. "And eat some fertilizer. You need something to make you grow. You're no bigger than a blister."

"Well, you should drink vinegar to make you shrink," Ancil said. "And prunes. Maybe they'd make you run faster. And look at those shoelaces. Some things maybe I can't help, like having red hair and freckles, but at least I keep my shoelaces tied."

Quick as an eel, he stooped and yanked her shoelaces loose. Just as quickly, she crouched and began to retie them. He tugged at her hair and then scurried to get in line for the cafeteria.

"What's for lunch, what's for lunch?" came the whispers from behind him in line. He looked ahead and saw pork chops, turnip greens, sweet potatoes.

"Mmmm, cinnamon rolls," he said when he spotted them. The cafeteria made their own cinnamon rolls, and they were scrumptious. As he ate, he looked around to see who wasn't eating what. No one was forced to eat anything, but if too many people left too many things, Mrs. Parker gave the "good nutrition" lecture or the "wasting food" lecture. Or both.

"You want my turnip greens?" Marcia asked.

Lloyd shoved his tray toward Marcia, and she expertly transferred the greens from her food tray to his. As he pulled the tray back, he saw Ancil staring at him.

"Want some?" he said. "They'll make you grow."

"Yuck," she said, shriveling her already small face. "They'll make you grow, too," she said. "The trouble is, you've grown too much already."

"But I have to eat a lot," he said, and some of his television knowledge popped right out of his mouth. "I have this disease called hypoglycemia." It was sort of like the opposite of diabetes. Since diabetics were supposed to be careful of what they ate, especially sweets, someone with hypoglycemia would, he presumed, have to eat a lot, especially sweets. "I particularly have to eat a lot of sweets," he said, taking a huge bite out of his cinnamon roll.

"Is it anything like leukemia?" Ancil asked, and Lloyd was surprised at the quietness of her voice. Her face had gone pale, and the freckles danced on her milk-white skin. Lloyd almost laughed at this reaction to his words, which he had not even intended to say. The shock of Ancil's response spread down the table until those farther away were whispering, trying to find out what had happened.

"Sh, sh. Hush!" Kirby told them.

No one teased Lloyd the rest of the day.

10

IN THE CAR LLOYD BOOSTED HIS FOOT ONTO THE
seat so Mama could tie his shoes. She looped the
laces into bows, revved the engine, checked the
traffic, and pulled away from the curb.

Suddenly Lloyd saw Ancil's scrawny pinched face
inside his head, and heard her voice. "At least I
keep my shoelaces tied," she had said. Mama called
him "Baby" with affection, but what would Ancil say
if she saw Mama tying his shoes? Ancil, Kirby,
Shafer, all of them would call him "Baby, baby,
baby."

So what did he care what they called him, anyway? And now they thought he had a serious illness! He smiled with pleasure at the thought of fooling them, however accidentally, with his superior knowledge. He slumped in the seat to escape the glare of sunlight from the hood of the car. Around two corners and they were home.

When Mama pulled into the driveway, she stopped the car but didn't get out. They both stared at the tree. The trunk had been severed and was lying in chunks in the dump truck.

"Now what are they doing?" Lloyd asked. The men were digging, by hand and by machine, around the base of the stub.

"They're going for the root," she said.

"Why don't they just cover the root and leave it there?" he asked.

"Because the root will rot and leave a sinkhole," Mama said. She pushed open the car door and trudged toward the house.

He ran to his room, flung his books onto his bed, then ran to the kitchen to watch Mama make the toast. The first two slices were already in the toaster, and she had the margarine slivered thin.

"Let me do it," he said, pushing next to her at the counter, taking a deep breath.

"Oh, go on," she said, smiling and nudging him

away. With one hand she snatched the hot toast from the slots, and with the other she dropped in two more pieces of bread. "Go sit at the table. I've already poured your milk." By the time she said those two sentences, she had spread the toast with margarine and jelly. She handed the sandwiches to him and ran to start changing clothes. How did she do it all so quickly? he wondered.

At the ball field she shoved her glove at him and sprinted around the field.

"Come on, Lloyd, run with us," Geneva said. He shook his head and concentrated on the warmth of the sun on his arms. He was hot enough already without stirring up his blood by running. "Come on, Lloyd, run with us," Geneva repeated each of the five times she circled the field, and he repeated the shake of his head.

"Okay, set 'em up, set 'em up," the women called to him as they finished their laps and scattered to their field positions for batting practice.

"Third base," he called out while the first ball was in the air coming toward him. Then, laughing, he bounded it down the first-base line. "Fooled you," he said.

"Pop-up to center," he said, and he popped up to the shortstop. "Over the fence," he shouted, and he bashed the ball. In a beautiful arch against the sky, it soared over the fence and landed in the meadow beyond. Finally, finally, Mrs. Parker knew that he wasn't the one causing all the trouble. Finally, finally, there was someone else to be chosen last.

"Come on, Lloyd, quit horsing around," Geneva hollered. Lloyd grinned at Mama, and she winked, echoing his good mood, his good feelings, and he was glad he had gone to school without a quarrel.

When Lloyd turned from fielding practice, he saw Kirby beside the bench astride the green-and-black spider bike. Lloyd tilted his head and grinned. Kirby shook his head.

"I didn't know," Kirby said softly.

"Know what?" Lloyd asked.

"You know. That you were, uh, sick."

Lloyd's mouth snapped shut. He had already forgotten about that. He shrugged, warm with the glow of it, like the respect a person gained by coming to school with an arm in a cast as though it were some brave and noble thing to break an arm or acquire a serious disease. He almost laughed.

"We don't have to talk about it if you don't want to," Kirby said. "But what I do want to know is why you won't hit the ball at school. I just don't understand it."

"It's my secret," Lloyd said firmly, from his new

position of strength. Starbursts of delight showered through him.

"Not any more. I already told everybody. And then you made a fool out of me."

"You made a fool out of yourself," Lloyd said. "And it's still my secret, isn't it?" He felt splendid with all his secrets. If Kirby thought he was a dummy, a real puppet kind of dummy who would do what Kirby wanted, then Kirby was the dummy.

"What do you do over here all the time?" Lloyd asked. "I don't see you playing ball."

"I have practice on Wednesdays and Saturdays. Other days I just ride around to see what's going on. I see some of my friends."

"Where's your mother?"

"Home," Kirby said.

"Home? You mean she lets you come here all by yourself?"

"Sure. I live right over there. It's just six blocks." Kirby pointed toward Lloyd's own house, except that Lloyd's house was only four blocks away.

"By yourself?" Lloyd repeated. What kind of mother would be so careless?

"You mean yours doesn't?"

"Well, we come back and forth together because of ball practice," Lloyd said, wagging his shoulders, shuffling his feet, not wanting to sound critical of Kirby's mother.

"So what's the big deal? Heck, I've always come back and forth by myself."

"Always?"

"Well, since I was seven or eight, anyway."

Lloyd traveled the distance in his mind, home and back, home and back. Sure. He knew the way. He even lived on the same street as the entrance to the park. He wouldn't get lost or anything coming by himself. And he knew how to look both ways before he crossed streets. For the first time, he thought about all the other children going back and forth to school. Back and forth. Alone. Or with each other. But very definitely without their mothers. He sat down on the bench suddenly, as if he'd been oofed in the solar plexis. He realized that he never left the house without Mama. Never, ever.

On the way home from practice, he held the olive shell in his hand, rubbing the cool, smooth shell until it adopted his warmth. "I'm going to start coming over here by myself," he announced.

"By yourself? Don't be silly," Mama said. "We both come at the same time and leave at the same time. It would be silly not to come together."

"Well, I could just come straight from school and meet you here." School was only four blocks from the Rec Park, too. In fact, school, home, and the Rec Park formed a triangle. An equilateral triangle, he thought.

"Yes? And what about your snack?"

He hadn't thought about that. Could he make it until supper without his snack? He rubbed the tip of his thumb across the pointed end of the olive shell.

"What I mean is, why don't you let me go places by myself? I'm old enough."

Even though she smiled, there was a vacuum between them, a lapsed space without air.

"Where would you want to go?" she asked.

"I might want to come play ball by myself sometime." Kirby was on some team or other. Lloyd didn't want to be on a team, but he could come over and toss a ball and chase after it and have the whole ball field to himself.

"You know I'll bring you over whenever you want to play ball. Haven't I always taken you anywhere you want to go?"

Lloyd struggled to think of what to say, how to say what he meant. "I mean, going places by myself. Like walking to school by myself. Like walking home from school by myself."

Impressions of things were plucking at his brain. All the things she did for him, all the ways she made him feel so treasured. Her love for him was like a warm, snuggly coat. But it was spring. It was too hot for warm, snuggly coats.

"It's dangerous," she said, as he'd known she would. "You might get hit by a car." She pulled into the driveway, and together they tromped across the dirt yard.

"But I know how to cross," he said. "I know how to be careful."

She went straight to the kitchen. "What do you want for dinner?" she asked.

Ready for the question, he answered quickly, "Breaded pork chops, lima beans, sweet potatoes, and applesauce." The pork chops at school were shriveled and made him hungry for Mama's thick, juicy ones.

He thought about how much she loved him. How when she was younger she had been so afraid of not being a good mother, so afraid of having him taken away from her. Always, when she came home she immediately went to do something for him. To fix his snack or his dinner.

"What's this all-by-myself stuff, anyway?" she asked when he was finished with his bath and wrapped in his blue velour robe. He sat in his green comfort chair trying to think up answers to her question.

At the table, when his plate was nearly empty,

she dolloped more onto it. "Want more?" she asked as though it were really a question, but she was already putting more applesauce, more beans on his plate. "Want my other pork chop?" she said, forking it from her own plate onto his. "What's this all-by-myself stuff, anyway?" she had also asked. She asked questions, he thought, without wanting answers.

"Twelve years old and you're already wanting to gallivant all over by yourself."

"Not all over," he said quietly. To school and back was not all over. To the Rec Park and back was not all over. "And twelve is old enough," he said.

"I take good care of you, don't I? Don't I take good care of you?" Playfully, she tweaked him under the chin.

With his mouth on the other pork chop, he muttered, "Yes, ma'am."

11

THE NEXT DAY, WEDNESDAY, WAS A TEACHERS'
workday. It was a holiday for the students. What a
relief! Perhaps he could manage school, he thought,
if he could take it two days at a time, Monday and
Tuesday and Thursday and Friday. Mama didn't
even wake him up for breakfast; she let him sleep.
He didn't hear her come into the room, but he was
aware of her good-bye kiss on his cheek.

At nine o'clock he woke up and sat stretching in
the bed for a few minutes. When he padded to the
kitchen and checked the refrigerator, he smiled.

There were two plates of sandwiches—his breakfast sandwiches and his lunch sandwiches. He heard the trucks chug-chugging outside, and he looked out the window. A cavern was enlarging around the old tree roots.

Still in his pajamas, he wandered to the front door and looked out, then went out to sit on the steps. He looked at the tree now, as though it were still there, piercing its branches into the sky. He thought about the things he had never noticed when the tree was alive and standing—the lacy pattern of the leaves against the sky, the broad shade they cast on the ground, the bony skeleton reaching, reaching after the lightning had killed it. He had never had anything to do with the tree before, not even to rake up the leaves.

Suddenly Kirby skidded up on his green-and-black spider bike. "Hey, I didn't know you lived here," Kirby said. "I come by here all the time."

Lloyd looked up, not knowing what to say, embarrassed about being in his pajamas.

Kirby said, "I've been watching them take down that tree."

"Yeah."

"Did you ever think the roots went that deep?" Kirby asked. "Of course, I know that tree roots usually go as wide underground as the trunk and limbs go above ground, but I just never thought about it, you know? It's amazing." Kirby shook his head. "They're going to fill the hole up, I guess."

"Yeah, I guess," Lloyd said. He hadn't thought about what they would do about the hole.

"Too bad. You could have a canyon in your own front yard! Hey, why don't you come on to the Rec Park with me?"

The question surprised Lloyd. He looked down the street toward the columns at the entrance of the park.

"I can't," he said. "Mama won't let me."

"Oh, yeah. I know. Because you're sick."

Lloyd had forgotten again, about what he had told Ancil. Hypoglycemia.

"Does it . . . does it make you feel bad?" Kirby asked.

Lloyd pulled his lower lip into his mouth between his teeth. What he'd told Ancil was a flat-out lie, and he'd never intended for anyone to make anything of it. It had just popped out. And it would be easy to tell Kirby right now that it was just a crazy joke. But he didn't want to. He liked the idea that they all thought he was ill.

"No, not really," Lloyd said bravely. "It just makes me weak. I don't have much energy. That's why I have to eat so much, to try to keep my energy up."

"Are you . . . are you . . ." Kirby couldn't finish the sentence.

"Going to die?" Lloyd said softly. Kirby nearly choked, and he waggled from side to side over the bicycle.

"Yeah," Lloyd said. "We all have to die."

"Want to ride my bike?" Kirby asked.

"I'm not dressed," Lloyd said.

"Heck, you can ride in pajamas. Here." Kirby swung a leg over and shoved the handlebars of the bike toward Lloyd.

"I don't know if I can," Lloyd said.

"I'll teach you, come on. I'll hold the back of the seat."

"I'm too big for you," Lloyd said.

"Nah. Come on. It's easy. Just hold onto the handlebars and put your feet on the pedals." Lloyd straddled the bike and gripped the handlebars. Kirby pushed the back of the seat. The bicycle wavered, and Lloyd kept touching his feet to the ground, first on one side and then on the other, frightened and laughing until he slid off the seat and planted both feet on the ground.

Kirby clapped him on the back. "I've got to go to

ball practice, but I'll come back later, okay?"

Lloyd swung his leg backward and up over the seat as he'd seen Kirby do. What a long smooth motion! He stood watching Kirby zip down the street, Kirby's body bobbing left, right, left, right as the pedals turned. Then he went back to the house to dress and eat his breakfast sandwiches. From time to time he interrupted himself to swing his leg up and back as if he were getting on and off the bike.

Wearing his favorite faded cut-off jeans and Georgia Bulldog T-shirt, Lloyd returned to the front porch to watch the digging. The pickup truck was parked in the yard, near the hole. A truck with a winch was at the curb, and the men were attaching a grappling hook to the tree roots. They were working down in the hole, out of sight. The hole was that big.

Lloyd poked the last of the last sandwich into his mouth and started down the steps to take a closer look. Then he realized he was barefoot. So? he thought, and started across the yard. The powdery dirt and the straggly clumps of grass were soft and cool beneath his feet. Over by the pickup truck he stood and watched. The men secured the grapple. The winch truck motor pulled the chain taut, but the remainder of the root didn't budge. Another man in the truck turned off the winch motor, and the men jumped back into the hole and dug around the root some more, chopping at it with axes. He could see, from the blunt ends where they had been cut, that the tentacles of tree root had extended themselves all around underground.

What fun it would be to play around the tree roots, down in the hole. Lloyd wished the men would not finish for one more day. Yesterday afternoon he could have enjoyed the last of the tree, but it had not even occurred to him. Only in his imagination could he now enjoy its shade or put a ladder to its trunk and build a tree house in the limbs.

He climbed onto the back of the pickup truck, legs dangling over the lowered tailgate, and watched as the men dug, and the winch pulled, in turn. As the winch motor stopped and started and the men changed the position of the grapple, the old monster tree began to release its final grip on the earth.

Lloyd lifted his legs, set his feet flat against the bed of the truck, and wrapped his arms around his knees. In the same instant, quicker than the grackle had snatched a crumb of bread, a link of the chain gave way. The release of tension flung the chain through the air so fast that Lloyd barely saw it coming before it struck the tailgate of the truck with a shattering crack. The truck bounced two feet across the yard.

In his cuddled position, arms wrapped around his knees, Lloyd didn't even fall backward. The chain fell to the ground with a few snapping writhes, like a dying snake, and then was still, seemingly harmless.

"My God, boy!" a man shouted, scrambling out of the hole and running toward Lloyd. "What are you doing here? Didn't we tell you to stay away?"

Lloyd sat still, certain that his heart had stopped and all his blood had petrified in his veins.

The man picked up the end of the thick chain. "A bit higher and it would have taken off your head!" He shook the end of the chain at Lloyd.

"Okay, okay." Another man came up. "Take it easy. He's not hurt, are you, son?"

Lloyd managed to shake his head.

"Bet it scared hell out of you, though," said the second man.

Lloyd nodded. He couldn't even make the words, "Yes, sir," start in his throat. His vocal chords were paralyzed, too. He'd been sprayed all over with Freezone.

"Scared the hell out of me, too," the first man

said. "God. If that chain had swung a bit higher it would have taken off his head."

"Thank goodness you didn't have your legs hanging over the back of the truck," the second man said. Lloyd's legs were still attached, he had his arms around them, and he wasn't hurt. Nonetheless, he could see his knees in bloodless stumps, severed as flat and smooth as the limbs of the tree had been, and his lower legs stacked, like cordwood, on the back of the dump truck.

Not at all sure his muscles would carry him, he slowly climbed out of the truck and wobbled across the yard. In the bathroom, he looked at himself in the mirror, amazed that he was merely pale and that the terror didn't even show on his face. He peeked through the window from time to time, as the men repaired the chain and tugged the last of the roots loose.

Kirby came back later and pounded on the door. "Come on out and learn how to ride the bike," he said.

Lloyd shook his head. "I can't."

"Aw, come on. You've got to have some fun, don't you?"

Lloyd was still speechless from the near accident. He thought of how Mama kept him home to keep him safe, how she was afraid of something happening to him in the street or at the ocean, and how the most dangerous thing of his life had happened to him right in his own yard.

"Why not?" Kirby rattled on. "You're dressed now, and you came out in your pajamas this morning. Do you need to put your pajamas back on so you can come out? I see they got the rest of the tree."

The men had cut the trunk in slices like so much bologna. One of the men walked over now, rolling a giant slice of the tree.

"I thought your mom might want this as a souvenir," he said to Lloyd.

Sure, Lloyd thought. A souvenir of the day I nearly got killed.

But Kirby said, "Hey, yeah, great," and leaped off the porch to touch the wood and stroke the grain.

"You had the tree in your yard so long, I just thought it would be a shame to haul it all away. A part of it ought to stay here, it seems to me," the man said, leaving the segment against the house.

"It must be a thousand years old," Kirby said. "Come on, Lloyd, help me count the rings."

"If by any chance she doesn't want it," the man said, "tell her to call us and we'll come haul it off for her." He held out a business card. Lloyd had to open the screen door to take it.

"Come on, Lloyd, help me keep track," Kirby said. Lloyd stepped out and sat down on the edge of the porch. His dangling legs reminded him of the pickup truck. He shivered and stood up beside Kirby.

"Here, keep your finger here," Kirby said, taking one of Lloyd's hands and guiding it to the wood. "Now don't move it. That's a hundred." Kirby lost count several times, but he didn't have to start over, he just went back to the nearest hundred where Lloyd was holding the place with his fingernail.

"Three hundred and sixty-two years old!" Kirby said. "Jiminy cricket! Do you believe that? Three hundred and sixty-two years old."

Lloyd was thinking that the tree had been more than a hundred years old when Georgia became a colony Maybe Indians had known this tree. And everyone who'd ever lived in Hanover had, perhaps, known this tree. There were many such trees in Hanover, huge live oaks draped with Spanish moss. He had never before thought about how long they'd been here.

"Come on," Kirby said, straightening up. He kicked the kickstand up and patted the bicycle seat.

Because he couldn't think of how to say no, Lloyd

swung his leg over and perched on the seat. He rode up the block and down the block on the sidewalk of Whitaker Street.

"Lloyd Albert, what do you think you're doing?" Mama called from the window of the car. He had forgotten to notice the time, forgotten to send Kirby away and be in the house watching television when she came.

"I've learned how to ride a bike, Mama," he said. She pulled into the driveway. With Kirby at his heels, Lloyd rolled up beside the car. "This is my friend Kirby," he said.

"Lloyd, don't you know you might have gotten hurt?"

"Oh, we were careful, Mrs. Albert," Kirby said.

Mama got out of the car and curled an arm about Lloyd's neck. She kissed the side of his head.

"I know, Mama," he said. "But I could get hurt anywhere." The chain sailed through his mind and landed with a *thwonk* at his feet. "I could get hurt anywhere."

12

AS SOON AS SHAFER CAME INTO THE CLASSROOM, A
hubbub began. Lloyd thought it had something to
do with Shafer's having been in the discipline desk
the day before yesterday. Shafer strolled up and
down the rows, ceremoniously placing envelopes on
some desks. Something funny was going on, something Shafer had written about the incident with
Lloyd, some revenge he was planning.

Shafer placed envelopes on every desk surround-
ing Lloyd's, but not on Lloyd's desk. Lloyd turtled
himself. When the bell rang, most of the class

continued to jabber and wave envelopes at one another as if the envelopes were the emblem of some secret club.

"Class!" Mrs. Parker called sharply. The clanging of the school bell had not brought them to attention, so she jingled a little bell on her desk. "What is going on? What are you doing, Shafer?"

"I'm giving out invitations to my birthday party," Shafer said from midway in one aisle.

"I don't think that's a classroom activity," Mrs. Parker said. "I assume, however, that since you are issuing the invitations in class, you are inviting everyone. But please sit down now."

Lloyd hung his head. He had not been invited. Of course, he didn't really expect to be invited.

At recess he scuffed his way toward the ball field. Before he had a chance to look down at his shoes, his name was called. He looked up and Kirby grinned, all friendly, and motioned him over. No, no, no, Lloyd wanted to scream. Amid the catcalls he shook his head slowly.

"Lloyd? You picked Lloyd first?" Bobby slapped his own head and fell to the ground.

"Yeah, I picked Lloyd first," Kirby said. "Come on, Lloyd."

Lloyd dropped his chin to his chest as he plodded toward Kirby. As the choosing went on, Lloyd noticed Ancil. She was so different from him. She stood with her head up, looking from one captain to the other as they called every name but hers. Watching Ancil, with her head held high, he could not lower his own. He'd show her. *She* was last now.

When he came up to bat, he accidentally clouted the first pitch, a high line drive that swooped over the second baseman's head. Kirby whooped with pleasure, and his teammates began the "Run, run, run" shout. Lloyd dangled the bat from his left hand and stared stupidly after the ball. A drop of sweat dripped into his eye. He brushed his forearm across his brow and cleared the damp, matted hair from his forehead. The center fielder fielded the ball, made the long throw to first, and Lloyd was out.

"Lloyd, Lloyd, Lloyd!" Kirby spouted the name like a curse. "No wonder Shafer didn't invite you to his party." Kirby kicked hard against the ground, then spat.

In the lunch line everyone was talking about the invitations.

"I got one."

"I got one."

"So did I."

Boldly they produced the envelopes as proof, envelopes they had hidden inside books or shirts.

By now it was generally known that only two people had been excluded. Lloyd kept his head inside his shell and shoved his mottled green tray along the silver rails of the lunch counter. The tray, hard and dusky green, became part of his shell.

Puny spaghetti-hair Ancil was the line leader. Lloyd watched her as she took her tray off the end of the steam table. Perhaps he'd call her rhinoceros nose. But when he looked at her nose, he saw she barely had one. Wart nose would be more like it. Wart nose and toothpick legs. He decided he would say it to her.

But when he slid his tray off the track, he saw that the other classmates had left spaces all around Ancil. Lloyd looked at her, sitting alone at the middle of the table. Their classmates were as much as saying, "If Shafer doesn't like you, then we don't like you, either." She looked so frail, so abandoned.

"Who cares," he said as he set his tray next to hers.

"Yeah, who cares," she said.

Words tumbled around inside his head. If he could find the right ones he would make it all right that they hadn't been invited to Shafer's party.

"When I said your hair is the color of spaghetti sauce, I meant it's a nice color. I mean I like spaghetti sauce."

"If it's something to eat, you like it," Ancil said. "You don't have to go around announcing it. You are a walking advertisement."

Be a turtle, he said to himself quickly. When he had seen her sitting there, so lonely-looking, he had forgotten to be a turtle. He had stuck his head out, and now it was bashed. All he had meant to do was be nice, to say something friendly. She had not listened to his meaning. She heard his words all wrong, like Mama heard his words wrong, like Mrs. Parker watched with the wrong eye. He wanted to pick up his tray and move to another place, but if he changed seats he would only be closer to those others.

"And I found out about hypoglycemia, too," she said. "If you really do have it, you're going to kill yourself because you are supposed to be very careful about what you eat. But I don't think you even have it. I think you just said it to get attention. People aren't going to like you just because you're sick, anyway. So there."

"So there, yourself," he said, glancing around in embarrassment, but they were isolated at the table and no one else had heard.

After lunch Mrs. Parker made things worse.

"I am sorry to say that I have learned that everyone was not invited to Shafer's party," she said. Lloyd stared at the initials carved on the desk. "I want you all to know that the classroom is not the place to issue invitations to a party unless everyone is to be included. I am disappointed, Shafer, that you were not sensitive enough to know you would cause hurt feelings by including some and excluding others."

Who cares, Lloyd thought. Whose feelings are hurt? Not mine. I wouldn't even want to go to Shafer's party.

For shared study period Mrs. Parker paired him with Ancil to review the multiplication tables. They would be outcasts together at the table in the back of the room. Ancil looked grim. As Lloyd plodded toward her, he matched her scowl.

"Eight times seven," she said as soon as he sat down.

"Fifty-six," he said, "and I did not say I had hypoglycemia in order to make people like me. I don't care if anyone likes me or not. Nine times nine."

"Eighty-one," she said. "And anyone who doesn't care if anybody likes them or not is either stupid or crazy. I do care if someone likes me or not, and I wish I didn't because no one does, anyway. Seven times six."

"Forty-two. Well, no wonder. You stand up to bat like a dumbbell and won't even take a swing at the ball."

"I've never heard of people not liking you just because you don't know how to play ball. Eight times four."

"It's my turn," he said. "Seven times four and how did you get to sixth grade without learning how to play ball?"

"Forty-two. No, I mean twenty-eight. You're getting me all mixed up. We don't play ball in our family. It's all girls in my family, or at least it was until we got a stepfather." Ancil paused in her rapid-fire speech. "That's why we had to move here. Because *he* lives here." She sighed, then resumed her spitball words. "But that doesn't mean we hate people who like to play ball. And what if I don't swing—at least I don't make an out, like some people."

"Girls play ball," he said. "My mother plays ball."

"That doesn't mean they have to. Nobody has to. There's no law."

She had this habit of looking directly at him that compelled him to look directly back. Her eyes were turquoise, like the color of the water in pictures of the Caribbean Sea, he thought.

"And if I did hit the ball I would at least have the good sense to run to first base," she said. "I learned that much just by watching."

"Well, give me a number. It's your turn." He wasn't going to explain himself to her any more than he had to Kirby. She could stand at bat the whole day for all he cared.

Mrs. Parker called for the end of the shared study period, and she told them to line up for a multiplication tables match. Study partners were on opposite teams. Mrs. Parker called the tables slowly at first, then faster and faster to try to mix up the ones still standing. Lloyd and Ancil were among those who remained standing no matter how fast Mrs. Parker called nine times seven, eight times nine, six times eight.

"I can certainly tell who was really working during study period," Mrs. Parker said. Because they'd been so close to fussing instead of studying, Lloyd looked across the room at Ancil, into her turquoise eyes, and each of them caught the other's laughter.

Emotions washed through him, hot and cold. How could he be enchanted with Ancil's eyes when he thought she was a pest and a runt? How had her splotchy face and flaming hair become the perfect set for those two turquoise gems? To call himself away from such unaccustomed thoughts, he drew the olive shell out of his pocket and cupped it beneath his hand on the desk.

"Hey, what's that?" Bobby asked. Before Lloyd realized what Bobby was talking about, Bobby reached across the aisle and scooped the olive shell from Lloyd's hand.

"Give it back," Lloyd said.

"I just want to look at it." Bobby held the shell up, turning it, examining the markings, the colors.

"I said give it back!" Lloyd spoke softly between clenched teeth.

"Make me!" Bobby said. Lloyd lunged across the aisle and grabbed the olive shell.

"Boys! Boys!" Mrs. Parker was striding down the aisle toward them. Lloyd sank back into his seat. "Lloyd, you give that back."

"It's mine."

"I saw you take it from him."

"But he took it from me first."

"What is it? What is it that's so important to fight over?"

Lloyd opened his hand to reveal the olive shell.

"Well, it's mine now," Mrs. Parker said, and she plucked it from Lloyd's hand.

He leaped at her, but her back was already turned. He followed her to the front of the room, shouting, "Give it back! Give it back!"

At her desk she opened the shallow center drawer, dropped the olive shell into it, and sat down, pulling her chair up so that her body shielded the drawer. He wanted to attack her savagely, to tear her apart bit by bit as a lion does an antelope.

Some trigger sprang his legs into action and propelled him not toward her but away, out the door and down the hall and down the stairs and through the outside door, on his downhill run, except that there was no Mama at the curb waiting for him.

13

WITHOUT STOPPING, LLOYD LOOKED BOTH WAYS
and crossed the street and kept on running until he
had crossed all the streets. He ran down the
sidewalks the whole four blocks home.

Only when he pounded up the steps did he
realize he couldn't get into the house. With a sigh,
he plopped down on the top step. This position was
fully exposed to the street, so he went around and
plunked himself on the ground at the back of the
house. He sat in the fringe of shade, leaning against
the sturdy concrete block foundation.

His blood was heaving, sloshing back and forth as though it had become an internal tidal wave. Cells and corpuscles were crashing and colliding crazily.

The striped cat eased through the fence at the back of the yard and stalked to the center. She stretched, turned three times and lay down in the sun. His hand scrabbled for a pebble or a clod, but there was neither in this soft, loamy soil. Digging at a clump of weeds with his fingertips, he upended the roots and tossed it at the cat.

"Scram!" he shouted, and Kitty-kitty jumped up and scampered away. "I don't want you," he said. "I don't want anybody."

But somehow he kept seeing those turquoise eyes, and the turquoise eyes got all mixed up with his feelings about the tree and about Mama, everything sloshing around inside with the cells and corpuscles. The word "stepfather" lingered. Just the one word, said with a sigh, and Ancil had revealed something. And he knew her pain.

There was a footfall and a shadow at the side of the house, and one of the people he wanted least of all appeared. Mr. Duggan. Towering above Lloyd, he seemed as tall as the house. Lloyd lowered his forehead to his raised knees and waited for the scolding to begin. Waited for the lecture and the talk about laws. There's no law, Ancil had said, but she was talking about playing baseball, not about going to school. Lloyd waited for the information about what would happen to him, where he would be sent. But there was only the whistle of a cardinal, the squawk of grackles, and the whir of a lawn mower from down the street somewhere.

After a while Lloyd opened one eye. Mr. Duggan was sitting, knees up, back against the house, just as Lloyd sat. One hand was open on his knee, palm up, and in the center of his palm was the olive shell.

Lloyd raised his head a bit, and Mr. Duggan moved his hand to offer Lloyd the shell. It was a trick. A trap. Lloyd stared at the shell, at the brown hash marks across the pale gray, blue, yellow, green background. With a quick grackle snatch, he plucked it from Mr. Duggan's hand.

"It must mean a lot to you, this olive shell," Mr. Duggan said.

Lloyd's blood went whoosh. Tidal waves again. A lot, he thought. The shell means a lot. The shell, the sand, the sea, that place of freedom. His second stepfather had been with them, he remembered, had taken them, in fact. It had been a happy day, a thoroughly fine day.

"I found it," he said, his voice muffled in his knees.

"You know, Lloyd, a lot of things in life are hard. But sometimes we cause ourselves more trouble than anyone else causes us. For instance, I have a new stepdaughter—"

Ancil, Lloyd thought, amazed at the coincidence. Mr. Duggan was Ancil's stepfather.

"—who is having the hardest time learning to like me. She's a beautiful girl, fourteen, long black hair. But she will not believe how much I care for her, how happy I am to have a daughter, even if she wasn't born to me."

No, it wasn't Ancil, wasn't spaghetti-head, Lloyd thought. But imagine. Mr. Duggan was a stepfather. Why didn't the girl like Mr. Duggan? But then, Lloyd realized, he hadn't liked Mr. Duggan very much, either. And he hadn't liked his stepfathers at all, not even the one who had helped him find the olive shell. Lloyd rolled the shell hard between his hands.

After a long while Mr. Duggan said, "It's five after three. If you let me take you back to school, you can sit in my car until three-fifteen. Your mother won't even know the difference. I don't see any reason to upset her about this, do you?"

Without another word between them, they walked to the car and drove to the school. When the bell rang, Lloyd trotted over to Mama's car.

14

AS LLOYD OPENED THE CAR DOOR WITH ONE
hand, he reached down and pulled a shoelace loose
with the other. In the car, careful not to look at
Mama, he retied the lace.

"How did you get your hand so dirty?" she asked,
looking at the dirt under his fingernails from where
he'd dug at the root of the weed clod.

"Oh, playing," he said.

At the ball field, when the women started their
laps around the field, he looked at them with
longing.

"Come on, run with us," Geneva said.

On Geneva's third time around he fell in beside her. Without breaking stride, she put a hand on his shoulder and they bobbed along in like rhythm for a few seconds. By the time they approached first base, she was ahead of him, rapidly lengthening the distance, and he was already breathless. But here he was running, he thought, when the day before yesterday he was nearly stripped of legs. He shuddered at the thought, and as Geneva headed down the foul line toward right field, he turned at first base and huffed his way toward second. At second base he turned toward third, amused about his shortcut but with no breath to laugh. His lungs roared with pain by the time he rounded third. Just as he crossed home plate, Geneva came alongside and patted him on the rump.

"Great going, kiddo," Geneva said, and she started around for her fifth and last time. How did she get around so fast? He wanted to smile at her, but his lips were pasted to his teeth. Sometimes he'd watched races on television, and he'd seen the runners collapse when they crossed the finish line. That's what he wanted to do now, but he puffed his way to the bench, instead.

Breathing in stiff snorts, he was still out of breath when they called for batting practice. Nevertheless, he stood in the batter's box and began cracking the balls. As his breath returned, his spirits soared. He'd run a lap! He'd run the bases. He pretended he was at school, zapping the ball over the roof of the building. Heads lifting higher and higher, his classmates would follow the ball with their eyes. And Ancil. He imagined looking at Ancil and grinning into her turquoise eyes.

"Lloyd, dadblast it!" Geneva hollered from behind him. "Will you quit sailing those balls over the fence! The only one who's getting any practice is you!"

With an effort, he brought himself back from the school yard to the Rec Park and kept the balls within the confines of the field. When the women were ready for their own batting practice, Lloyd began another lap around the field. Alternately he ran, then walked, all the way around the outfield this time. His legs, his lungs, his throat, his head were all on fire. Glorious, flaming pain and joy.

"Well, you certainly look happy," Kirby said as Lloyd plopped onto the third-base bench.

"Oh," Lloyd puffed. "It's you." Spreading his knees, he dropped his whole upper body between them.

"Well, I'm fixing to make you even happier,"

Kirby said as Lloyd gulped for air, then spurted it out.

Kirby said, "You're invited to the party."

Lloyd could only hear in rhythms of his own breathing. Huff. Puff. *You'reinvited. Totheparty.* Kirby's message came in two parts, on the inhale and the exhale. *You'reinvited—totheparty.*

"You're invited to the party," Kirby repeated. "I told Shafer that I wasn't coming unless he invited you."

All Lloyd could do was stare. Kirby wanted him to come to the party? Shafer's party? Kirby wanted him to come? Lloyd wanted to go to the party even though he did not want to go to the party.

"What about what you said today at school?" Lloyd asked.

"I didn't really mean it," Kirby said.

"Are you teasing?" Lloyd asked.

"No, of course not," Kirby said. "I said I wouldn't come unless you were invited. He's going to call you after your softball practice."

"Are you doing this because you think I'm sick?" Lloyd remembered Kirby's sympathetic looks, the feeling of being a hero because he'd said he had hypoglycemia.

"Of course not. Lloyd, I'm trying my best to be

friends with you, but you just won't let me. Want to ride my bike?"

Lloyd leaned back against the chain link fence. The diagonal squares pressed into his flesh, and sweat dripped from his eyebrows into his eyes. Being a turtle was easier, more comfortable. But he kept seeing Ancil with her head held high on her scrawny neck.

He looked at Kirby and at the green-and-black spider bike. Here he was, actually sitting and talking with one of his classmates. He smiled, all friendly-like, and smiled at himself smiling.

He stood up and reached for the handlebars. Kirby pushed him to get him started. Lloyd pumped the pedals and rode around the perimeter of the field.

In the car going home, he said, "Mama, Mama, I really can ride a bike."

His words created the vacuum between them again, but in a minute she said, "I know. I saw you."

"I can ride a bike," he said again. There was so much he wanted to tell her, but his words were tied in double bowknots and they wouldn't come loose in his mouth.

"What do you want for supper?" she asked as they walked toward the house.

"You fix what you want," he said, hugging her,

then opening the door for her. "You choose."

In the tub the water lapped against his body, warm and soft. When the water was only a few inches deep, he began to bathe, and he emerged in his robe before she called him. When Mama saw him, she looked up with surprise, and her lips drew thin and white for a moment before relaxing into a smile.

Without stopping at his green comfort chair, he went straight to the buffet, removed the place mats, and put them on the table. "Mama, if you reach the plates for me, I'll put them on the table," he said.

He could reach them as well as she could, but he was so afraid of dropping them. Silently she handed him the plates. He took two forks from the drawer and rolled them each in a napkin and placed them to the left of the plate. When she put lasagna on the table and reached for the serving spoon, he took it from her.

"You sit," he said. "I'll serve you." Trying to remember how she did it, he scooped up a spoonful of lasagna. The mass slipped off the spoon and splatted onto the table.

Surprised that she had not jumped up to help him, he held his left hand against the spoon, scooped the hot lasagna from the table and plopped it onto his own plate. Then he ran to the sink for the dishcloth and stuck it and his burning hand under a cool stream of water. He returned to the table, swiped at the mess and smeared it. She sat silently, watching. After two trips to rinse the dishcloth, there was no trace of lasagna on the table.

"Put the plate right next to the serving dish," she said as he again prepared to serve her. She pushed her plate until it bumped the dish of lasagna.

"Oh," he said, looking at her and grinning. Her eyes were light brown, the color of a little coffee in a white cup. Like his own, he thought. This was his day for noticing eyes.

He spooned lasagna onto her plate, not in the neat squares she managed, but he didn't spill any this time. Then he pushed his own plate close and put lasagna on it and sat down.

"Thank you, Mama," he said.

"For what?"

"For letting me do it."

By the time the telephone rang, he had almost forgotten Shafer and his party.

"I won't come unless you invite Ancil," he said, surprised at the idea and at his boldness.

"Good grief," Shafer said. "Who's Ancil?"

"The new girl. The one with red hair." Lloyd imagined Shafer's shoulders drooping, and he raised his own.

"Then that will be everybody in the class," Shafer said.

"So?" Lloyd said. Even over the telephone Shafer's sigh was clearly audible.

"Oh, all right."

Mama was looking at him with curiosity. The only phone calls he ever had were from Granny or one of his aunts or uncles.

"I've been invited to a birthday party," he told her. "It's at the Rec Park tomorrow after school." Already his mind was searching for an appropriate present, one they could afford.

"Can I give him a softball?" Mama almost always had an extra ball, in case they lost one.

"Yes, you may give him a softball." She stared at him for a moment, then pulled him to her. "Oh, Lloyd, Lloyd, Lloyd," she said into his hair as she hugged him. The hug, he knew, was for more than softballs and birthday parties.

15

AS SOON AS LLOYD STEPPED INTO THE SCHOOL
yard, Kirby collared him, saying, "Lloyd. How
could you!"

"How could I what?"

"Tell Shafer that you wouldn't come to the party
unless he asked that red-haired wart."

"Ancil? Do you mean Ancil?"

"Who else?"

"But *you* told him you wouldn't come unless I
came."

"That's different. He's my friend. I stuck my neck

out for you," Kirby said. "Whether you go or not is your own business."

"But I'm going, I'm going," Lloyd said. There seemed to be a need for some kind of reassurance that Kirby had not stuck his neck out for nothing. "That is, maybe I am. *If* he invited Ancil." He hadn't thought of it that way when he talked to Shafer last night, but Lloyd guessed that he'd stuck his neck out, too.

"He invited her," Kirby said in disgust and walked away.

Lloyd found Ancil in the hallway outside the classroom. "Have you heard anything about Shafer's dumb old party?" he asked her. If Shafer hadn't really invited her, he didn't want to cause more embarrassment.

Ancil made a dry spitting sound. "I wouldn't go to his party if he asked me sixteen times," she said.

"Did he ask you?"

"He made up some story about running out of invitations yesterday," she said. "It's the first time I've been invited to anything since I moved here, but I wouldn't go to his party if he had gold medals for prizes. And I told him exactly what he could do with his old party."

"You did?" He was astonished and amazed and pleased and disappointed all at once. Why hadn't he had the courage to tell Shafer what to do with his party? "But you're going, aren't you?"

She made another dry spit. "You must be crazy," she said.

Well, he thought to himself, echoing Kirby's words, I said I wouldn't go unless she was invited, and she's invited. Whether she goes or not is her own business.

At recess Kirby stubbornly chose Lloyd first again. This time Lloyd held his head high and boldly stalked over to stand by Kirby. He met Ancil's eyes and winked. She stuck her tongue out at him. When they came to the last and still didn't call her name, she walked away. Lloyd expected some tattler to holler, "Mrs. Parker, Ancil's not playing," but no one said a word. Either they didn't notice or they were glad to be rid of her.

When he came up to bat he was so tempted. He looked at the roof of the school building and imagined the ball sailing clear over the top. Reality stopped him. The building was two stories high, and he would be more likely to break a window than to clear the roof.

Waiting at the sidelines, Kirby clapped his hands and smiled. "Come on, Lloyd, baby," he said.

The first ball was pitched and Lloyd swung widely. His teammates groaned. Lloyd glanced at

Kirby. Kirby was not groaning, but his eyes had lost their hope.

"Come on, Lloyd, baby," Shafer said from the pitcher's mound. "Kirby says you can really hit the old ball." Lloyd swung at the second ball and made his second strike. He was not going to let Kirby control him.

"Come on, Lloyd, baby," Shafer teased. "Let me have it right here." Shafer smacked the ball into his glove, then fired it toward the plate. Lloyd heard Geneva shouting inside his head. "The harder they come, the harder they go!" He reared back with the bat, sliced the air hard and level, and connected solidly with the ball. The ball shot back to Shafer. Shafer reached for it with a surprised look and was knocked over backward.

"Was that where you wanted it?" Lloyd asked.

Shaking his hand from the sting of it, Shafer held up the ball to show he'd hung on to it. Lloyd was out. He dropped the bat and went to find Ancil.

She was sitting leaning against a tree, and Lloyd sat down beside her. As with Mama yesterday, all kinds of things were going around in his head, but he couldn't push anything out of his mouth. He reached into his pocket, then held out the olive shell.

"I want you to have it," he said quietly. The

turquoise eyes darted at him. "It's an olive shell. A lettered olive. See the markings, in rows, like letters? That's why they call it lettered. I don't know why they call it olive."

"You want me to have it?" Ancil said.

He nodded, smiling at the way her eyes widened as she reached for it. "And I want you to come to the party."

"No," she snapped, withdrawing her hand. "I'm not going to any party. I don't want to go to any old party."

"Yeah, I know. I don't either. But it's the first time I've been invited to anything, too. I just started having friends. Kirby just started being my friend."

"Really?"

"And I really do want people to like me," he said. "In fact, what I want is for everyone to like me. To think I'm fantastic." He laughed at himself. "Stupid, huh?"

She shrugged and took the shell from him and turned it slowly in her hand.

"Do you see all the different colors? It appears to be only brown and gray, but if you really look you can see yellow and blue and green. See?" They both stared at the olive shell until Mrs. Parker's whistle sounded. Lloyd held out a hand to Ancil. "Will you come to the party? I'll be your friend. And Kirby will, too, I bet."

She stood up without taking his hand and she walked away without answering.

"Ancil, I'm trying to be friends with you," he said, echoing Kirby's words again, "but you won't let me."

She turned on him with narrowed eyes and narrowed lips. "You started the hatefulness, remember?"

And now, he thought, she had his olive shell. He had given it away for nothing.

16

AFTER SCHOOL MAMA DROVE LLOYD TO THE drugstore to buy wrapping paper, ribbon, and tape. He selected some paper with all kinds of balls on it—baseballs, footballs, basketballs, soccer, tennis, and even golf balls. At home Mama set the softball on the table beside the wrappings.

"I don't need a snack today," he said. "We'll have refreshments at the party." She started toward the bathroom to change out of her work uniform. "Will you wrap the present first?" he asked.

"I thought you were the boy who was going

to do everything himself," she said.

"Mama, you know I can't do everything. Just some things. I just want to do the things I can do."

From the doorway she gazed at him for a moment. "You can do this if I show you." She rolled out the paper onto the table and flip-flopped the softball box across it, showing him how to measure paper for the box. She held her finger on the paper while he taped the sides of it together, and she showed him how to square the corners on the ends. He taped an orange bow on the top.

"That's a fine job," she said, tousling his hair.

"Now I'm going to walk to the Rec Park by myself," he said.

His words stunned her. "No," she said. "Absolutely not."

"Mama, it's only four blocks."

"Lloyd, no. You're asking too much. You're doing this too fast. I put my foot down." And she put her foot down.

"And I put my foot down, too," he said. Then, before she could stop him, he picked his feet up and bolted for the door.

"Lloyd Albert, you come back here," she said. "This is ridiculous. We're going to the very same place."

But he was already out the door, already walking

across the dusty yard and down the sidewalk toward the Rec Park. This was the very sidewalk where he'd learned to ride a bike just two days ago. This was the very sidewalk in front of his own house, and yet he did not know it any more than he had known the tree. He knew about the Alps, but he did not know his own sidewalk.

He heard the car chug to a start behind him, saw it as she drove alongside him on the opposite side of the street. Eyes down, he studied the lines and cracks of the pavement.

"Lloyd, now you get over here and get in this car," she said. He could feel her sigh, feel the car sigh, feel the whole world sigh, not wanting to let him go.

"No, Mama," he said. "But I'll ride home with you after."

She drove along slowly opposite him. But when he reached the entrance of the Rec Park, she touched the tips of her fingers to her lips and blew him a kiss.

The party group was gathered near one of the ball fields. Lloyd was disappointed to see that they were going to play ball at the party. He should have known. Shafer would rather play ball than eat. Lloyd added the wrapped softball to the pile of presents heaped on a picnic table.

"Since it's my birthday, I'll be one captain," Shafer said. "Kirby will be the other."

"Surprise, surprise," Marcia said, because Kirby and Shafer were almost always the captains. Lloyd saw Ancil at the edge of the group. So she did come, he thought, and he strolled over to stand with her.

Shafer had first choice, and he chose Bobby. Then Kirby chose Lloyd. Lloyd sighed. There was Kirby choosing him again. For the first time ever, he was getting a little control over his own life, and he wasn't giving any of it to Kirby.

An even number of kids were at the party. Shafer had first pick, so the last choice was left to Kirby.

"Call her name," Lloyd whispered to Kirby. "Do it!" he said when Kirby hesitated.

"Ancil," Kirby said, but the name was lost in the storm of complaints.

"No fair, no fair," a shout went up from Kirby's disgruntled teammates. "It's not fair to have Lloyd and her on the same team."

"Tough luck," Shafer said.

"Shut up," Kirby said to the grumblers.

When they lined up for batting order, even though he'd been chosen first, Lloyd put himself in last place, after Ancil. With fourteen kids on each team it took several innings to get to the last of the batting order. Shafer's father told them to play four innings or until everyone had had at least one turn at bat.

Ancil came up and stood there, like always.

"Give her a base on balls," someone said. The team in the field changed the chant from eh-eh-eh-eh-eh-swing to a rhythmic and taunting eh-eh-eh-eh-eh-*don't* swing.

"You know we don't give bases on balls," said Bobby.

"We don't have Mrs. Parker's whistle, either," Marcia said.

"Here we give bases on balls," Shafer said. "Go on," he said to Ancil.

"What does that mean?" Ancil asked.

"It means if you get four bad throws you get on base free," Kirby said. "Go on down to first."

"But she hasn't had four bad balls," someone from Shafer's team protested. "She's had sixteen good ones."

"Same thing," Shafer said. "Sixteen good ones equals four bad ones and I don't want to stand here all day."

"Besides, we're ahead four runs and Lloyd's last batter," Bobby said. Ancil trotted to first base.

"Come on, Lloyd, baby, hit for me," Kirby

pleaded as Lloyd came up to bat. "Show 'em you can do it." Even though Kirby was trying to be a friend, Lloyd was not going to let Kirby have power over him.

"Come on, Lloyd, baby, hit for me," Ancil called from first base. She had one foot against the base and the other a step forward, proud to be on base and all revved up to run. His eye roved the familiar field where Geneva had so often complained about his hitting balls over the fence. Shafer wound up and let the ball go. As soon as the ball was in the air, the groans began.

"Don't swing at everything," his teammates begged.

Shafer's team chattered, "Eh-eh-eh-eh-eh-swing."

Bringing his arms around on a slight upswing, Lloyd put all his weight into his arms. The ball cracked off the bat and rose over Shafer's head and kept rising and rising until it disappeared in the glare of the sun.

"Holy spit!" Shafer said, turning to follow the arc of the ball. Lloyd's teammates were all yelling their usual, "Run, run, run," but he stood there, holding the bat and staring after the ball. He'd done what he wanted. He had not left Ancil stuck on base. He watched the ball curve over the center fielder's head and begin falling, falling, falling until it landed in the meadow beyond the fence.

Then he caught sight of Ancil's spaghetti-sauce hair bouncing as she rounded third. Boy, the little runt could run! Something about her movement drew him like a magnet. Lloyd dropped the bat and started heaving his way toward first base.

"Holy spit!" Shafer said again. Except for Ancil and Lloyd, the twenty-six classmates stood frozen. Like they'd all been sprayed with Freezone, Lloyd thought, as he jiggled his way toward second.

Suddenly Kirby leaped up from the bench, whooping and hollering and slapping his legs. "I told you! I told you!" he exploded.

As Lloyd ran toward third, he had to hook a thumb into his belt to hang onto his pants. He was losing his baby fat.

The game was over. Shafer's team had won by two runs, but it didn't matter. Everyone jumped around and clapped Lloyd on the back just like when anyone else hit a homer.

Shafer's mother called them for refreshments. Together they galloped to the table where Shafer's father handed out cold drinks. Then they split the air with singing "Happy Birthday" while Shafer's mother cut the cake and his dad plopped ice cream on top. Lloyd thought he'd ask for just cake, or maybe just ice cream, but there was no way to manage it without calling attention to himself. The next time he hit a homer, he wanted them to be able to boost him to their shoulders.

Clutching his plate, he looked around for Ancil. His eye caught a glimpse of tall, blond Mr. Duggan crossing the parking lot with a tennis racket under his arm.

"Hey, Mr. Duggan," Lloyd yelled as loud as he could. When Mr. Duggan turned and saw him, Lloyd called, "I just hit a homer!"

Mr. Duggan's mouth opened and his head lifted in surprise and pleasure. He raised one arm and waved victory fingers.

There was someone with Mr. Duggan, and it was a girl with long black hair. Lloyd smiled double and waved victory fingers back at Mr. Duggan. Then he spotted Ancil sitting alone on a stone bench.

"Boy, can you run," he said as he joined her.

"Boy, can you hit!" she said. She held up the olive shell to show him that she had it with her. He wanted to point out Mr. Duggan and the black-haired girl, wanted to say something about stepfathers, but he didn't know how, didn't know her well enough yet.

"Boy, did you surprise everybody," Kirby said,

coming over and putting one foot up on the bench between them, spooning ice cream and cake into his mouth as if he were in an ice cream-eating contest.

Lloyd hunched one shoulder. He didn't know what to say. It was as though, by hitting the homer, he had given away a part of himself.

"Want mine?" he asked Kirby, holding out his plate. The ice cream was already melting, forming a pool around the cake.

"You don't want it?" Kirby said, hesitant but eager.

"Nah. I'm not supposed to eat it," Lloyd said.

"Because of your—?"

Lloyd shrugged. Let Kirby think what he wanted. He saw Ancil lower those turquoise eyes, rub her thumb against the olive shell, and hide a grin. Sometime soon Lloyd would straighten Kirby out, but not now. A person had to have some secrets.